Miss
Smithers

ALSO BY SUSAN JUBY

Alice, I Think
Alice MacLeod, Realist At Last

SUSAN JUBY

Miss Smithers

Harper *Trophy* Canada™

An imprint of HarperCollins *Publishers*

Published by HarperTrophyCanada™, an imprint of HarperCollins Publishers Ltd

Originally published in trade paperback: 2004
This mass market paperback edition: 2005

HarperTrophyCanada™ is a trademark of HarperCollins Publishers

HarperCollins books may be purchased for educational, business,
or sales promotional use through our Special Markets Department.

HarperCollins Publishers Ltd
2 Bloor Street East, 20th Floor
Toronto, Ontario, Canada
M4W 1A8

www.harpercollins.ca

Library and Archives Canada Cataloguing in Publication

Juby, Susan, 1969-
Miss Smithers / Susan Juby. – 2nd ed.

ISBN-13: 978-0-00-639527-0
ISBN-10: 0-00-639527-9

1. Beauty contests – Juvenile fiction. 2. Teenage girls – Juvenile fiction.
3. Maturation (Psychology) – Juvenile fiction. 4. Diary fiction. I. Title.

PS8569.U324M57 2005   jC813'.6   C2005-902411-9

OPM 9 8 7 6 5 4 3 2 1

Printed and bound in the United States

For Dr. Bill Juby

ACKNOWLEDGMENTS

The author gratefully acknowledges the support of the Canada Council for the Arts.

Many thanks to my mother, Wendy, who is an unfailing source of support and always has been; Greg McDiarmid, still my target market; Hilary McMahon, agent extraordinaire; Ruth Katcher, who asks all the right questions; Lynne Missen and Lisa Berryman for their support and enthusiasm. Thanks also to Gail and Karl Hourigan, Sandy Thompson, McDiarmids of all stripes, Trevor Juby, Aaron, Scott, and Carl Banta, Kathy Waring, Elizabeth Murphy, Ian Whitehouse, and all Miss Smithers contestants, past and present.

And a very special thanks to James Waring, who never fails me and never fails to make me laugh.

A VERY SPECIAL GIRL

January 10

I am a special girl. It was my mother's suggesting that I'm not that decided me. I mean, really, that's not the kind of thing you want to let pass unchallenged.

I already suspected that this would be the year I would bloom, the year I would graduate from the ranks of the marginal into the realm of the practically normal (or even slightly above average), and today's events confirmed it.

My dad's friends Finn, Marcus, and Kelly came to visit this afternoon, and before they'd even cleared the door, Finn told us he had important news to share.

"You'll all be impressed to hear about my new endeavor," he announced grandly.

Finn joins everything. He's a member in good standing of every club Smithers has to offer–the Legion, the Curling Club, the Rotary. He's convinced that it helps his business. He sells used sporting goods and does very well at it, so maybe he's right.

"I am the newest member of the Smithers Rod and Gun Club."

My dad burst into laughter, shooting coffee out his nose, spraying Marcus and the opposite wall. My mother's back stiffened.

"The Rod and Gun Club?" asked my father when he'd recovered somewhat and Kelly had mopped up the explosion with a paper towel.

"You bet!" crowed Finn, thrilled with his own unpredictability.

The thought of Finn in the ultramacho Rod & Gun Club was a little strange, given his well-known lack of athletic ability.

"Did you know they put on wild-game dinners?" he asked his assembled audience.

My mother snorted her disdain from the stove.

Kelly weighed in with a worried question: "But are you going to have to shoot a gun?"

Finn looked offended, conveniently forgetting the cast he'd had to wear for six weeks after dropping a bowling ball on his own foot, the damage he'd done to the felt top of every pool table he'd ever been near, and various other mishaps related to his lack of hand-eye coordination. Of course, all his friends, my father included, were equally incompetent in the sporting arena, but at least they didn't try.

"Of course I'll shoot. But in case it doesn't go well, I figure I'll help them out with my connections."

Because I was speculating that maybe he could give a seminar on how to establish a record-breaking bar tab, I didn't hear what he said next, but my mother's response was unmistakable.

"Not a chance in hell!"

Now this was interesting. "What?" I asked.

"Don't even repeat it, Finn. She is not interested." My mother was adamant. Furious even.

Finn turned to me, leaking empathy.

"I was just saying that my brother and sister shooters are looking for a very special girl for a very special job."

"She's not doing it!" said my mother.

Marcus chose this moment to contribute to the conversation.

"You know, Diane, it's a great learning experience for a young woman. Personally, I really enjoy the competitions."

My mother shot him a death-ray glare and

hissed, "I'm sure you do, Marcus. I think we all know how you feel about young women."

Marcus's mouth snapped shut. His tendency to date younger women was a sore spot between him and my mom.

Finn ignored them both.

"Yes, only a very special girl will do. A very special girl who wants a clothing allowance of four hundred dollars."

Oh my God. With $400 I could clean up in every United Church and Salvation Army thrift store from here to Vancouver.

"Do you think you might be that special girl?" Finn asked me.

"Yeah. Probably."

"She is not a special girl!" interrupted my mother.

He ignored her. "Because not just anyone can be the Rod and Gun Club representative in the Miss Smithers Pageant."

Miss Smithers Pageant? And here I thought it was just a simple endorsement deal, like maybe I'd wear a Rod & Gun Club T-shirt until they found someone who could fill it out better.

My mother, an evangelical, vegetarian, peace-

4

activist feminist, couldn't stop protesting, even though I'm sure she knew it would only drive me into the arms of the enemy.

"Why doesn't one of the, the . . . killers' daughters do it?"

"The *athletes'* daughters all have other commitments—like shooting competitions and hockey practice," Finn replied.

She snorted, triumphant.

"Right. They have productive things to do. They are too busy being *people* to be *Miss* anythings!"

Made sense to me. I mean, I'm not exactly overburdened with commitments. As long as I leave one night a week free for the family Monopoly game, I can probably fit the pageant competition into my schedule.

"What do I have to do?"

I felt like a special forces agent being brought in to support the troops.

"Oh, you know, go to a few town events, get your hair done, that sort of thing." Finn leaned in close and whispered, "And spend that four hundred dollars any way you want."

January 11

I admit I never imagined that the Miss Smithers competition could be in the cards for me. It's an important rite of passage for half the girls in town, at least half of those between the ages of sixteen and eighteen who don't have a full-blown public speaking phobia. But I am not most girls. Until recently I have been Alice Pariah MacLeod, world record holder in the Most Embarrassing Moments category.

After a series of unfortunate social failures in first grade, connected to my mistaken belief that I was a hobbit, I was pulled out of school to be educated at home. Here is a recipe for becoming a total misfit: Get run out of grade school for being delusional, then spend ten years talking to no one but your parents. Add a liberal helping of ineffective counseling. Then transfer into an alternative school in which you actually stand out as being reasonably high functioning. And presto! You have a weirdo.

In spite of these handicaps, there seems to be increasing evidence that, as I age, I can not only begin to fit in, I can even excel in certain areas, such as personal expression via fashion experimentation.

Besides, the Miss Smithers Pageant, in spite of what my mother might think, isn't really a beauty contest. Oh sure, everybody looks presentable enough. I mean, nobody's totally hideous or anything. From what I can tell, it's more about how good you *are* than how good you *look*. You have to be the right kind of good, too—churchgoing but not aiming for the priesthood, nice but not a brownnoser. The contest has about six hundred events and is just vague enough for every girl in town to figure she's got a shot at the title—if she can just figure out what it means to be a good girl.

I doubt very much that I'm a good girl. For one thing we aren't churchgoers. My parents are basically pagans or at the very least heathens. And for another thing I go to the Alternative School. Everyone knows that's only for people with issues. Good girls don't have issues; at least they don't have the kind of issues that require that they attend nontraditional educational institutions. Plus I've been in counseling for a long time. Good girls don't need counseling. They usually *are* counselors—at summer camp and places like that.

So why would I consider entering the pageant? Well, one thing I do know is the value of a dollar. Like I said, there are so many events in the Miss Smithers competition that there's got to be room for everybody to excel in at least one, even if it's just, like, night bowling or something. And maybe being so not good will be an advantage. I'll stand out for being different.

My confidence has been boosted by the fact that I haven't had a serious personal setback in months. I haven't been beaten up since last summer. I haven't been busted trying to make out with Goose, my sort-of boyfriend, since that fateful day we met last fall. On the two occasions I've seen him since then, my parents have kept us under heavy surveillance. He lives in Prince Rupert, which is several hours and a few towns away, so we don't get to see each other often or for long.

I've been receiving education outside the home quite a few months now. I even take a few classes in the regular school as well as at the Alternative. No one has covered me in pig's blood at a school dance, probably because I haven't dared go to a school dance yet. And my counselor, Bob, is really coming along. His voice is still low and intimate and he still looks quite tortured, but he's been practically cheery lately. Working with a success story like me has been good for his self-confidence.

Concrete proof that I'm practically normal these

days is that just last week my parents had a party for my sixteenth birthday and there were people there who were not blood relatives. One of them was even my age!

My mom was there, of course, resplendent in a shapeless dress and her very chunkiest jewelry. She was pretty much beside herself that I was willing to let her have a party for me. She was so excited, she made the birthday cake with sugar rather than the usual cane juice, in flagrant defiance of hippie vegetarian dietary laws. Will the good times never end?

My dad was also pretty pleased to be at a non-traumatic event involving his only daughter. When he asked me to dance to Van Morrison, he looked as though he couldn't believe it when I said yes.

My brother, MacGregor, was there with one of his little science club friends. The two of them stood around in their funny cords and too-small sweaters looking prepared to answer any and all questions that might come up about the life cycle of the aphid. God, I love my brother. I danced with him when my parents played my Folk Implosion CD to show me how much they cared.

Finn, Marcus, and Kelly made an appearance too. The three of them danced together to "Islands in the Stream" by Dolly Parton and Kenny Rogers and looked far too comfortable doing it. Finn has the distinction of being the only openly gay man the town of Smithers has to offer. Marcus's claim to fame is that he drives the only cab in town and, even though he is not rich or a musician, somehow manages to date very young women. (My theory is that his young women are all on a budget and trying to save on cab fare.) Kelly doesn't really have any claims to fame. He is very gentle and sensitive and makes MacGregor, who is eleven, look worldly by comparison.

Even my counselor, Bob, whom I secretly refer to as Death Lord Bob because of his Satan-is-my-fashion-consultant black clothes and small, pointy beard, stopped by. He was thrilled by my willingness to socialize and enjoyed taking full credit. He seems not to have realized yet that with my increasing normalcy, he might soon be out of a job. Oh well, I'll probably keep seeing him anyway, because although I am firmly on course, particularly fashionwise, he is just beginning to hit his stride as a therapist. I want him to be able to bask in the light of his one success story. I doubt the Teens in Transition (Not in Trouble) Center, where he counsels, will provide him with many other career triumphs. He slouched around the party and, as usual, seemed to be irresistible. I caught both my mom and Finn checking him out. At one point I think even my friend George was giving him the eye, at least until I elbowed her.

George (her real name is Georgette) is my best friend. More accurately, she is my only friend. But even if I had two, she'd be the best one. I met her on a trail ride last fall. One of her cowboy-wannabe brothers was found in a compromising position with my drug-addict fashion-plate cousin from Vancouver. In all the chaos, we got to know each other. She's like me in that she doesn't buy into that bubbly, happy-girl stuff. But unlike me she is competent in several areas.

While I have undergone a radical personal transformation in the last year and become quite fashionable, George shows no signs of changing, at least outwardly. She still wears jeans and plain shirts and has no-nonsense hair. She looks sort of like how I used to before I started making an effort. George is interesting in that she doesn't seem to care about appearances. She can't help it. It's just not her nature.

George is high up in the 4-H organization, which I think is cool, even if she doesn't. She's won several cow-husbandry championships and made it to the provincial competitions twice. She focuses on cows as a form of minor rebellion (her parents are in pigs). They've worked it through as a family, though, and now her parents have accepted her choice of livestock. George wants me to join 4-H, so we can go to competitions together, but except for MacGregor's tropical fish we don't have any animals. I feel like I'm more of an urban person than a rural one. Even though I'm from Smithers, British Columbia, population 5,000, I am probably destined for life in the big city. You can tell from my magazine collection. I've got every issue of *Spin* dating back almost a year, ever since my parents got me that subscription. But I do envy George her competitive outlet. It must be nice to have a place to shine. I find my family to be an unappreciative audience for my talents.

Other than city mouse/country mouse type differences, George and I are on the same wavelength. My mother calls us the "disaffected duo," but it's obvious that she's pathetically grateful that I have a friend at all, seeing how up until now I haven't exactly been the picture of popularity.

I think George had a good time at my party. She danced with MacGregor's friend. At one point she gave him a little hip check, which sent him flying into my mom's spinning wheel. The wheel is supposed to give guests the impression that she's incredibly earthy and crafty and more or less lives off the fat of the land. Of course, she's never once used it. George should be more careful. She does a lot of chores and other manual labor and doesn't know her own strength.

The only person missing was Goose. He was going to try and come to my party, in spite of the distance involved, but his truck died earlier that week because he forgot to put oil in it and the engine seized. Goose is not mechanically inclined.

My mother refers to Goose as my boyfriend, even though he's not really. She calls him that to everyone she talks to, especially since she found out his parents are both scientists with Ph.D.s and his brother, Colin, is starting his doctorate. My mother loves any association that might reflect well on her family. I guess she's hoping some of it will rub off on us. She's so impressed by Goose's family's educational accomplishments that she's almost managed to forget her first introduction to him.

Goose and I met at a fish show in Terrace. Our brothers were showing fish and we ended up sort of getting together, which I know is not entirely normal, in terms of an appropriate romantic setting and everything. Dignified people our age get it on in movie theaters and in strangers' bedrooms at parties, not in community center cloakrooms. And normal people don't get caught by their parents just as they are rounding first base. That last part would probably be why my mother thinks Goose and I are boyfriend/girlfriend.

I guess we *are* sort of boyfriend and girlfriend. He's cute, you know, with messy blond hair and devil-may-care clothes, and he's unself-conscious, which I admire. He's also got this personal magnetism thing that I can't resist. At least not in person. But on the phone, which is how we spend most of our time, he doesn't have the same effect on me. Which is good, because I don't like the sappy way I get around him. I can't stand the idea that I'm not captain of my own ship.

I do like Goose, though, and not just because I'm better than him at everything except for bargain shopping. His lack of excellence is actually one of his nicest qualities. Every super-achieving, Rhodes scholarship-winning, concert piano-playing, five language-speaking family needs a failure to help lower expectations. Goose is his family's loser. I would be mine, if my parents weren't such underachievers. I just don't know how serious Goose and I are as a romantic unit. It's hard to keep the flame alive long distance. After all, he lives in Prince Rupert and I live in Smithers. That's practically a world and four hours of fast driving apart.

Even though he couldn't come, Goose sent me a present—a pair of mittens that look suspiciously like a reject Christmas gift from an elderly relative. Goose is very good with his money, which means that his gifts are not the kind that make you feel all guilty and beholden. He once made me an entire bouquet of flowers made of rolled-up newspapers. I imagine they left his bank account more or less intact. I put them in a vase in the living room, but my dad accidentally used them to start a fire. I keep meaning to find a second grader to whip me up a few more in crafts class.

My other gifts were pretty good. Finn makes good money selling used sporting goods, but he squanders it on liquor, and Kelly and Marcus are the original no-money men. I was amazed that the three of them bought me a dress, and believe it or not, it's very nice. It's one of those Chinese-style dresses with a mandarin collar. Very vintage looking. They said they got it for next to nothing on eBay, and you've never seen three men look prouder. Kelly even started to cry a bit when I said I liked it. Luckily Finn got him calmed down before he spoiled the party atmosphere.

George gave me a gift certificate to Stereo Sam's so I can pick out a CD. I'll probably have to special-order one, because my taste in music favors the alternative and hard-to-find.

Finally, Mom, MacGregor, and my dad got me exactly what I asked for: three notebooks and the complete works of Ted Conover. He's an intrepid journalist who does amazing things like ride the rails with hoboes and pretend to be a prison guard or a migrant worker and then write about his experiences. I know getting books isn't like getting a car or something, which is what some sixteen-year-olds get for their birthdays, but my family is quite poverty-stricken. My dad is an ex-musician and a mostly unpublished writer, and my mom is the assistant manager at the local New Age/secondhand bookstore, so we aren't exactly raking it in. Mom also runs a small candle-making operation in the basement, probably to give my dad some paid employment, and I have high hopes that the company will pay for a few consumer items like those found in the homes of wealthier families. Post-1972 furnishings would be nice.

In the meantime, I like my very modest gifts. I enjoy writing and have been thinking that a Conover-inspired career as a daring journalist might be an option. I'm not planning on any dangerous adventures, or even leaving home really. Living with my family in Smithers, B.C., may just be adventure enough.

I think I'm going to use my new notebooks to start a 'zine. Smart, interesting people my age are always writing 'zines. Ted Conover probably started out writing 'zines. In case you've been living under a rock and are completely out of touch, putting out a 'zine involves writing and publishing stuff that's very personal and that only you really care about. Like maybe there will be three other people in Kansas or someplace who are also interested in your subject. A 'zine is the perfect training ground for the budding journalist, especially one who keeps a diary.

Much like Ted Conover, I won't shy away from writing about the dark underbelly of life, the side you don't see on network TV. I'm innately drawn to unusual subcultures, despite my ability to participate in very mainstream activities such as the Miss

Smithers Pageant. To aid me in my unrelenting honesty and search for the truth, I've come up with a pseudonym, or *nom de pen*, as they call it in the trade: P. J. Hervey. The name is a tribute to my favorite alternative musician as well as a nod to my wild side. No one is as alternative and cool as P. J. Harvey. You will note that I changed one letter in her name. It's subtle, but I think it works. It will also be my defense if she comes after me legally for semi-impersonating her. Who knows—maybe if I almost use her name some of her coolness will rub off on me.

My party went until nine P.M., when George's parents came to get her. My parents' party went until three in the morning, when my dad finally convinced Finn and Marcus and Kelly to go home.

January 12
My Miss Smithers candidacy and successful birthday party may not sound like much, but when I think back, I realize that I've come a long way. Until recently most of my socializing involved dodging spitballs in class and trying to outrun would-be attackers. My friendship with George is a giant advance for me. For a while there, it was looking as though my inner circle was only ever going to consist

of my parents and younger brother. When I was still being taught at home, I tried befriending the other homeschool kids, but it didn't work out due to the fact that most of them were even stranger than me. When you're as marginal as I am, you shouldn't spend time with people who could push you right over the edge into total freakdom.

MacGregor's the only genuinely together person in our family. He's been in normal school from kindergarten and is really the glue that holds us together. We all try to take our cues for how to behave from him. When faced with a crisis, which happens quite often in our family, we sit very still and watch to see how Mac reacts. Sure, it's a lot of pressure for a young kid, but I'm sure he prefers that to letting us follow our natural instincts, which are always to overreact and make things worse.

In some ways George is a bit like MacGregor. She doesn't get too excited about things. In comparison, I feel always more or less hysterical, even if I don't show it. George is a calming influence. We don't see each other that often because she lives in Houston, B.C., which is about forty-five minutes away. It's lucky for us that Sausage Place is famous throughout the Bulkley Valley Lakes District, or I wouldn't get to see her as often as I do. Her parents, like most of the adults in the region, make the trip into Smithers at least once a month to buy sausages. They probably have an extra pride of ownership because at least some of the sausages are filled with their own pigs. As I mentioned before, George's parents raise pigs, which has been tough on her self-esteem, even in a place like Houston where quite a few families raise pigs. Several large sows are painted on the side of their truck along with the farm logo: Heller Hogs. Somebody painted over the "er," so now the truck says "Hell Hogs." George always has her mom and dad drop her off at our house before they head into town. Just because she's not hysterical doesn't mean she's not sensitive.

Anyway, our early visits were a bit awkward because we were both sort of inexperienced in the hanging-out-with-friends department.

The first time she came to visit, we spent the first hour sitting in silence in the living room. My mom came scurrying in every few minutes with some new health food horror she'd concocted.

"Hello!" she cried brightly, thrusting a tray at George. "Earth clod?"

After George gingerly took one, my mother

went swirling back into the kitchen, apron ties flapping. Seconds later she was back with another tray.

"Soy milk?"

We'd only just gotten rid of the Earth clods under the couch cushions when my mother materialized yet again.

"Oh! You've already finished your cookies—wheat free, dairy free, and unsweetened, if you can believe it!"

Before she could crack out the wheat germ wafers, I gave her the look—the one that any sane person would recognize as very dangerous, but which my mother manages to ignore half the time.

This time she got it and left immediately.

From my place on the couch I saw her start back into the living room at least twice and turn back, finally forcing herself to leave us alone.

Then of course George and I had nothing to say to each other. You'd think, with us being teens, socializing would come naturally, that we'd just automatically start talking and giggling up a storm and doing each other's hair. Not so. All we managed that first visit was "Hey" and a nod at each other now and then.

Eventually, the deafening silence got to be too

much and I asked George if she wanted to listen to music. She looked relieved and nodded yes. I put on my new P. J. Harvey CD and turned it up nice and loud.

Mom passed by a few times, obviously wondering what was going on. She may have said something, but I couldn't hear her over the music.

That worked out well. Since the music was too loud to talk, we picked up books and started to read. It was quite fun, really. Almost like being alone.

Still, I was relieved when George's parents came to get her. All that heavy socializing can be tiring.

George called later to say what a good time she'd had. We talked for over an hour.

Once we figured out that we liked the same things, our visits got easier. When we get burned out from all the togetherness, you know, after an hour or so, we just retreat into our books, only speaking now and then to make fun of something. We've had some good times, George and I.

During our phone conversation tonight, I told her about my 'zine idea. She was very supportive and said I should send a copy to Ted Conover. Her favorite Conover book is the one where he lives with Mexican migrant workers. Mine is the one where he goes to Sing Sing. I didn't tell her about the pageant yet. I'm not sure she'll approve. In fact I know she won't. She doesn't even approve of that Conover book where he lives in Aspen with the rich people. If she thought that was a cop-out, I can't imagine what she'd say about me enrolling in the Miss Smithers Pageant, even if it is for journalistic purposes.

Goose called, for the second time in three days. This was unusual, because he keeps himself on a tight phone budget. We used to e-mail, until he downloaded some virus that wiped out the hard drive on his computer. Now we talk three times a week, after six P.M. and on weekends. I guess I can't complain, because if I was paying, we'd have to send smoke signals. When I told him about the pageant, he was happy for me but distracted. I thought he'd make a bigger deal of the fact that he is now dating a candidate, but he seemed to have other things on his mind. He's hoping to visit soon and is already worried about whether his truck is going to make it. He's been really affectionate on the phone lately, saying embarrassing things like "I can't wait to see you again," and "I just want to spend time together."

He may miss me, but there's no excuse for that kind of talk. I mean, that intimate stuff is all right as long as it's spontaneous. If I thought he was *thinking* about it all the time, I would be so disgusted. I happen to know from my research that boys think about doing it every four seconds on average. That's oppressive.

When Goose and I are up close and personal, there's no stopping us, other than with a bucket of cold water or close personal supervision, which is basically the same thing. But the whole actually having sex thing—I don't know about that. It's a big step and one that I plan to take with my eyes closed. Or maybe I'll go all Conover about it and treat it like research. You know, be detached.

January 13

My mother has been attempting maternal guidance. Her unsuccessful efforts have revealed the fascist tendencies just below the surface of most New Age practitioners and cemented my commitment to civic participation. If I wasn't already entered in the Miss Smithers contest for personal growth and financial gain, I'd now be in it for spite.

This afternoon she sidled into my room with her treasured copy of the antipornography learning-aid video *Not a Love Story* clenched in her hand.

Here we go.

"Alice . . ." she began. "I have decided that if you are so much in need of money that you are willing to demean yourself by entering some . . . some beauty competition, I think your father and I should step in."

I waited.

"We will give you the four hundred dollars."

"You'll give me the four hundred dollars?"

"Yes. We feel strongly enough about this that . . . We feel strongly about this."

Lie. Total lie. *She* feels strongly about this. My dad couldn't care less.

"So you will pay me four hundred dollars *not* to enter the Miss Smithers contest."

"Well, not exactly. We will pay you the money so you don't *have* to enter."

"That's bribery."

"Alice. Shit." She was getting frustrated now. "It's not bribery. It's concern. We've spoken before about the exploitation of women."

She was about to give me *Not a Love Story* when I held up my hand.

"Mother—Diane—that's about pornography. There's a slight difference between that and a good-citizenship competition."

She was starting to lose it now.

"There is not!" she thundered, and pointed an accusing finger. "Why are there no boys in the Miss Smithers Competition? Hmmm? Because it's sexist! That's why!"

She put the hand holding the video to her stomach and the other on top of her head in an effort to settle her chakras.

"Look. Let's investigate beauty contests together. We'll read about them, maybe watch one." She looked sick at the thought. "And"–she floundered–"you'll see that they are bad!"

Oh great. Not another women's studies project with my mother.

"Look, Mom, I mean Diane, I'll find out for myself. The best way. By entering one."

She clutched her video to her chest. "But you'll. . ." Her voice broke off. "Okay," she whispered.

Suddenly I felt bad.

"It'll be like that woman you're always telling me about, you know, that Gloria Steinem woman when she worked at the Playboy Bunny Palace."

My mother brightened a bit.

"But we could just read about beauty competitions," she tried again.

I gave her a look. "Diane." And shook my head.

As she walked out the door, I called, "But I'm still willing to take that four hundred bucks."

She gave me a dirty look.

My mother has never been very good at explaining politics.

MEET THE SPONSORS

January 14
I had my first meeting at the Rod & Gun Club tonight, so they could give me my money and so Finn could get his Brownie points for finding them a candidate.

He picked me up after dinner. As I got into his car, he looked me over.

"What have you got on?"

I looked down at myself. I was wearing my Miss Rod & Gun Club introductory outfit. I'd chosen it carefully, and I thought it struck a nice balance between hip and appropriate to the occasion. I wore a cropped green camouflage T-shirt and army pants with boots. To emphasize my Miss Smithers qualities, I wore a belt with lots of silver, my largest earrings, and very red lipstick.

"What?" I asked him.

"For God's sake, don't you have, like, a dress or something? You know, something from the Gap."

I just glared at him and buttoned up my old general's coat.

"Christ, *I've* got more feminine outfits than that," he groused under his breath as he pulled out of the driveway.

For a badly dressed person, Finn isn't shy about commenting on other people's clothes. Why is it so many people who have terrible taste like to pretend they're just above it all? Finn is the perfect example. He considers himself this supremely tasteful guy and says the only reason he surrounds himself with tackiness—his clothes, his car, his friends (my dad excepted)—is that no one in Smithers could possibly *appreciate* his great taste. He likes to give the impression that if he moved to New York, he'd suddenly lose the vinyl loafers, Finning Tractor jacket, and pilled polyester dress pants and morph into Mr. *GQ*.

I am quite sensitive to fashion problems since I had them myself until not long ago. I used to be a plaid-shirt-and-jeans person until my cousin Frank, who visited last summer, inspired me to establish a unique fashion identity. Frank is from Vancouver and positively reeks of fashion, even though her life is not exactly one of deep thought and good actions. I admire that.

To give him his due, Finn *has* updated his look recently. He has taken to wearing track pants wherever he goes. They make quite a tasteful statement with his tasseled loafers, let me tell you.

"How many third world workers were exploited to make your pants, Finn?" I asked, just to change the subject and see his reaction.

"Look, sweetheart," he said, "don't think I don't know about the global economy. I read *No Logo*. That's why I sell used sporting goods, not new."

Finn has to be the most adaptable person in the world. That point was proved when we got to the clubhouse and he transformed into He-man of the Bush Land.

"How the hell are ya!" Finn shouted to the Rod & Gunners as we got out of the car.

They were a rugged-looking group with unruly beards scraping across woolen undershirts, except for the odd clean-cut, wild-eyed guy in business casual with an American accent.

Finn was in the thick of it, pumping hands and slapping backs and acting like he'd just returned from cutting down an eighteen-point buck in the prime of its life after having parachuted into the bush and subsisted on roots and snowballs for a month. From his demeanor no one would have guessed that he is a man who basically lives on A&W and bar snacks.

Inside the clubhouse, a plywood shack with tin siding applied to deflect stray arrows and bullets, everyone settled into their seats for the meeting. A fellow who looked like he might be a first-degree relative of Sasquatch stood in front to run the meeting.

"Today we'll be covering a lot of ground—permits, regulations, a discussion of civil disobedience, and a presentation on barbecuing wild game by Arnold."

Arnold, a giant of a man in red suspenders, ducked his head and blushed under his beard. A smattering of applause.

"But first, our newest member, Finn Calhoun"—more applause—my mother's women's circle could learn a few things about supportive atmosphere from these guys—"has brought along a guest he'd like to introduce."

Creaking of chairs and whisper of beards across vests as the shooters turned to get a look at me.

Finn stood up.

"Hello! Hello!" he bellowed. "After a long, hard

search I am pleased to introduce a young lady, a close personal friend of mine, who is willing to run as the Miss Rod and Gun Club candidate."

"Stand up. Stand up!" he whispered, giving my leg a covert kick. Reluctantly I got up and stood there with my arms folded, with what even I knew might be interpreted as a sullen look. I should have known better than to put myself in a position to be rejected.

Who would be the first to make a rude comment?

Silence for a fraction of a moment, and then the place exploded into applause, or at least that's how it sounded to me. They were practically throwing their John Deere hats in the air and snapping each other's suspenders. They liked me, they really liked me! And I hadn't even won yet.

Hard as I tried, I couldn't keep the smile off my face.

When the clapping died down and the grins subsided back behind the mustaches, Finn introduced me formally.

"Gentlemen"—loud ahems from the floor revealed a few well-disguised women—"and ladies," he continued, "I am pleased to introduce to you Alice MacLeod. Miss Rod and Gun Club."

January 15

Being a Miss, like any other performance-oriented activity, is an art into which one must plunge oneself.

My mother thinks the competition's all about conforming to a sexist version of what makes a woman. I would argue that it's about celebrating the candidates' inner excellence and outer fashion sense. To that end, I plan to spend the shooters' $400 very carefully. I'm not just going to buy up every pair of leg warmers from here to Burns Lake. I'm going to be discriminating.

I finally told George about the pageant. She wasn't impressed. She couldn't believe I'd signed on for the Rod & Gun Club, and needlessly pointed out that my family is militantly vegetarian and my mother is one of those violent pacifists who riot over the slaughter of baby seals and approve of bombing medical labs that do animal research. George said she could never see herself entering a beauty pageant.

"They're sort of stupid, don't you think?"

I found myself getting defensive.

"Not completely. I mean, there's the money. And the experience."

"I thought you were just doing it for irony. So you could write about it in your 'zine?"

"Well, yeah. But you don't have to make it sound so, you know, dumb."

She sighed heavily. "Whatever."

When I tried to smooth things over and talk to her about how strange Goose is being, she acted like it was no big deal.

"Guys are like that."

How would she know? She doesn't have any more experience than I do. George and I seem to have developed this competitive vibe. She seems to resent it when I give her fashion advice. I resent it when she talks to me like I'm a shallow know-nothing. What's happening to us? I thought friendship was supposed to be fun and easy.

Maybe I'm just nervous and irritable because the first Miss Smithers event is next week. I don't know exactly what will happen, but the organizer who called me said we have to dress up and be ready to say a few words about ourselves. I feel sick every time I think about it. Maybe I have one of those public speaking phobias you hear about all the time. Finn said not to worry and that it'll be good for me to get a look at the competition. Fine for him. He drinks. Plus, he doesn't have to go to this event because it's for candidates only.

I'm not sure entering the Miss Smithers contest was a good idea. Now I understand why none of the Rod & Gun clubbers' daughters was willing to run. It should really be one of them going through this to atone for all that wildlife killed by their throwback fathers. A born-and-raised vegetarian like me doesn't deserve the stress. I'm a former homeschooled child. I don't have the social skills.

Later

I just got home from my counseling appointment. Bob wasn't much help, because as usual he's having personal trouble. Maybe he got dumped. He's one of the most sought-after males in Smithers, so I'm sure he'll have no trouble finding a replacement.

I have no idea what women see in Bob. Sure, he's got that deep growly voice that asks all those probing intimate questions. But he's *too* sensitive. As Jack Nicholson once said: He can't handle the truth! I've made it my mission to tell him only the positive things going on in my life so he can feel good about himself. It's basically a community service that I provide.

When I dropped the news about the Miss Smithers Pageant at the end of the session, it was like

I'd announced that I was putting on a Broadway play and he was being cast in a starring role. He got to his feet and began pacing, running his hand through his black hair to make it more picturesque.

"Are you serious? That's fantastic. Just fantastic! So tell me about it. When do we get started?"

Oh God. I hope this doesn't become another disappointment for him. He doesn't need any more pressure in his life. Between all the professional and romantic failures, I'm probably the only thing keeping Bob afloat.

THE HOMESCHOOLED ADVANTAGE

January 19

In a development that may bode well for my chances, it turns out that the reigning Miss Smithers is herself a former homeschooled child! I know all this because she told us quite a bit about herself at tonight's Meet the Queen event. In fact, most of the evening was taken up with the outgoing queen baring her extra-white teeth at us while patting her extra-large curls and trying not to weep. She told us that the contest was going to be the high point of our lives. "Except for the lucky girl who wins the title," she said. "Her life will be transformed for one whole year."

When one of the girls asked what being crowned queen entailed, soon-to-be-former Miss Smithers, actually crying now, sobbed, "Well, you get to leave the house quite a bit."

She pulled herself together, fixed her mascara right in front of us, and tried again to tell us about the competition and the duties of the candidates and queen.

"And if you are blessed enough to win"—her voice began to crack—"you will represent the town of Smithers"—tears welled up in her eyes and cut a swathe through her makeup as they traveled down her cheeks—"at a variety of events." Then for good measure, she repeated, "And you get to leave the house all the time." With that she broke down completely.

Seeing that Miss Smithers was unable to continue, Mrs. Martin, a tidy lady in a pink sweater set, who is the official pageant chaperone, took over.

"There, there, Heather." She patted Miss Smithers's heaving shoulder. "It's very emotional for the queens when they have to step down."

"But at least I've still got the Lord," sobbed Miss Smithers.

"That's right, Heather. You've still got God."

Two candidates in front of me looked at each other. One whispered, "Do you go to church?"

The other replied, "I do now."

Mrs. Martin continued. "Heather was the Home School candidate last year. Do we have another representative from that organization this year?"

At first no hand went up, but after a long pause, one hand emerged reluctantly just over its owner's head.

"You're the Miss Home School candidate this year, dear?"

The girl wore a floor-length flowered dress and a baby-blue cardigan, and had her hair in a French braid tight enough to stretch her eyelids toward her ears.

She spoke so quietly no one could hear her.

"Mumfmmfmf," she said, and we all leaned in closer.

"I'm sorry, dear. I don't think we heard that," said Mrs. Martin.

"I'm the Unschooling candidate." The girl's voice was nearly inaudible. One of the candidates behind me whispered, "Good. There's at least one person I can beat in public speaking."

"Is that what the Home Schoolers are calling themselves this year?" Mrs. Martin asked.

"Mmffmfmm."

"Sorry?"

All I caught of the next sentence was ". . . split. Into the Unschooling Collective and the Deschooling Association."

Mrs. Martin's perfectly lipsticked smile hung on her face like a piece of wet laundry, and she put a hand to the cream-and-pink scarf around her neck.

"So do we have a Deschooling candidate with us here today also?"

Tentatively, another hand rose from the crowd and another girl, nearly identical to Miss Unschooling, but wearing a pale-yellow cardigan, stood. She opened her mouth as though to say something. Nothing came out, and looking shocked, she closed her mouth and sat back down quickly.

"Welcome, dears." Mrs. Martin didn't register surprise at having two mute clones from the splintered homeschool community in the competition. I gave a little thanks that I was no longer part of that crowd. I mean, I'm not exactly regular school material or anything, but the Alternative School's at least *near* the high school. All the homeschool kids I've met are either deeply religious or the children of hard-core hippies, neither of which is ideal for preparing a girl to be crowned queen. (The current Miss Smithers being both the rule and the exception.)

The Meet the Queen event was held at the local real estate office, which is, according to Mrs. Martin, a "big supporter of the pageant." I heard several of the girls complain that launching the competition there gave Miss Northern Real Estate an unfair advantage, but one of the candidates pointed out that it didn't matter because we weren't really being judged tonight.

"This is just to weed out the freaks," said the candidate who'd expressed an interest in starting to attend church.

"What do you mean?" asked the girl beside her.

"Well, if someone is, like, totally hideous or, you know, insane or something, they try and get rid of her here, before anyone sees her."

"Get out," said an unbelieving candidate to my right.

"It's true. We don't even find out who some of the judges are until, like, the last night."

"Isn't that illegal?"

A candidate in an unfortunate lime-green

sweater who was sitting to my left added, "Yeah. And I heard they totally, like, spy on you at work and stuff."

"So we're going to get secret-shopped at our jobs? That would suck. It's bad enough when the company sends out spies. At least those secret shoppers have low expectations. The pageant people might not understand that I'm always like a total bitch at work," said a hopeful with an odd arrangement of pigtails all over her head.

"No shit. And it gives the losers an advantage because they never go anywhere. Like those home-school chicks. The only place they go is church, and no one's allowed to spy on them there. It's like a safety zone or something," said Lime Green.

Several girls around me nodded in outraged agreement. The Unschooling and Deschooling candidates shrank further into their cardigans.

This was getting ugly. Not at all what I expected from people competing for the title of best girl in town. And what exactly did they mean by losers who never went anywhere? I never went anywhere. Surely they didn't mean me!

Fortunately, Mrs. Martin returned from escorting Miss Smithers to the washroom, where she could fall apart in private, and resumed explaining the rules and schedule before the gossiping could get worse.

"Girls, throughout this pageant you are to conduct yourselves as though you have already won. Decorum is key."

A candidate somewhere behind me asked, "Is that makeup? Or would that be more like jewelry?"

"From now until the end of the competition you are not only representatives of your organizations, you are ambassadors for the town of Smithers and its merchants."

I looked around. Smithers and its merchants were in a lot of trouble if we were the best they could come up with. I'd seen most of the girls around the high school, but some must have already graduated because I'd never seen them before. Not to be rude or anything, but the majority of them weren't the kind you'd want advertising your business.

I knew the contestants wouldn't be like Miss Universe contestants or anything, but I thought that at least they'd look respectable. Sure, some did. Miss 4-H looked like a farm girl, which was fine. She was clean-cut and glowed with health, but she had unusually large biceps. I could see them through her coat. Even George didn't look as strong as Miss 4-H, though they both had that ruddy complexion that says "I spend too much time outdoors."

Several of the other girls didn't look healthy. Miss Loggers' Association, in her jean jacket and runners, had the hard-bitten appearance of a heavy drinker. Miss Main Street looked, forgive me for saying it, trashy. Her hair was too big for comfort, and I'm sure she had to use a pulley and lever system to get her pants on. I'd seen her before, hanging around with the tough head-banger girls who loved to make my life unbearable. Anyone who would hang out with the eyeliner brigade doesn't deserve the title of candidate, as far as I'm concerned.

I don't know how most of these girls, who look like they could barely drag themselves to the next bush party, are going to manage the hectic pace of the Miss Smithers Pageant and its many citizenship events. Miss Moricetown, the Wet'suwet'en candidate, looked fit and attractive enough, but she's obviously political. She was wearing a T-shirt with a picture of an armed standoff at a blockade on the front. The caption underneath read: "Coming soon to a neighborhood near you."

Overall, I was disappointed in the caliber of the competition. Only Miss Unschooling and Miss

Deschooling looked like good girls. And Miss Ski Smithers looked not only good but also good looking. She smiled and pretended she didn't hear when the other girls made mean remarks. She was fashionable but classic in her dove-gray sweater and her charcoal wool slacks and patent leather loafers.

The rest of us seemed to have miscalculated somewhere in our outfits. Like me for instance. I thought my brand of thrift-store chic would mark me as both a woman of the people and a stylish dresser, but next to Miss Ski Smithers in her tasteful outfit, I just looked ratty in my wool plaid A-line skirt, saddle shoes, and green V-neck sweater with only a few holes where you could barely notice them. I think Miss Ski Smithers' sweater may actually have been cashmere but couldn't be sure, since my parents are underemployed and things like cashmere sweaters are not a part of our lives.

I was the only candidate who attends the Alternative School. But in no parallel universe could that be considered an advantage.

How on earth did I get myself into this? I comforted myself with the thought that at least I got fired from my job at the New Age bookstore last summer, so I can't get secret-shopped.

At the end of the evening Mrs. Martin had us introduce ourselves and say a few words. Most girls barely managed to say their names and sponsoring organizations. The mute stay-at-homes were too shy to say even that. They just smiled and hunched their shoulders up around their ears. I was so nervous, I said something along the lines of "malicemacleodrodandgunclubrep."

But one girl, Miss Bulkley Valley Fall Fair, whose trying-too-hard skirt and suit jacket suggested a fiercely competitive nature, volunteered that she likes dancing and pizza, thereby making the rest of us appear as though we lack public speaking skills. Then we were given a handout with a copy of the pageant schedule and went our separate ways.

I am disappointed that my involvement in the competition isn't more fraught with irony. From the looks of it, more than a few girls in this contest are doing it for the clothing allowance money. (Lord knows some of them could use it.) I had assumed that everyone would look the same, dress the same, be the same: meek, appropriate, boring. Except for me, that is. I assumed I'd be the standout entry, the intriguing dark horse candidate. I guess I'll just have to establish my individuality through my unique behavior and talent.

We'll certainly earn our money. Besides Meet the Queen, we have to survive having our pictures taken for the paper, an etiquette workshop, a fashion show, a charity curling bonspiel, a mother-daughter tea and speeches, a talent show, and the big finale, the Sweetheart Ball, where the winner will be announced. I'm exhausted just thinking about it. Thank God things don't really get going for another month. I never paid much attention to the pageant before. Probably no one does except the people in it. It's amazing anyone is willing to do all this for a contest where winning means you get to ride around on a threadbare float twice a year and cut the ribbon for the new Boy Scout hut.

I was really looking forward to telling George about it tonight on the phone, but before I got the chance, she told me her news. She lost her virginity at a 4-H rally last weekend! I couldn't believe it. I mean, I could believe someone would want to do it with George. She is my best friend, and accordingly attractive, but I thought she'd at least call me first or something. The truth is that I thought I'd lose mine first.

She said it happened quite suddenly. No doubt. My mother gave me a copy of *Our Bodies, Ourselves*, so I've read the medical literature.

George said they were in a workshop discussing vitamin supplements and worming schedules when she noticed one of the guys looking at her. I asked her if he was attractive, and she said, "I don't know," as if it wasn't even a consideration. It was a two-day rally, and they both happened to be billeted at the same house. You'd think that an organization dedicated partly to breeding domestic livestock would realize the dangers of a coed sleeping situation, but apparently not.

During dinner they flirted, which, knowing George, probably involved her raising her eyebrow and giving him a sardonic look. This guy must be the Fabio of 4-H or something, because later that night he snuck into her room and one thing led to another and now she's part of the been-there-done-that crowd. The guy even brought a condom! I asked her if that wasn't a little presumptuous—and not very flattering if you think about it—but she didn't seem to mind. She said, "At least I didn't have to use mine. Those things cost money."

She didn't go into much detail about the actual experience, and just snorted like it was no big deal when I asked. Her blasé attitude was probably connected to the fact that she grew up on a farm and became acquainted with the facts of life at an early age. Even so I was a bit put out.

This isn't going to sound very nice, but I felt jealous. After all, Smithers is much bigger than Houston, B.C., so I'm more of a city person than George. Everyone knows that city people have sex sooner. And I'm the one with a sort-of boyfriend who shows signs of being obsessed with sex. I'm also the one with the highly developed sense of style. It just doesn't seem quite fair.

In the end I didn't even bother to tell her about the event tonight. It just doesn't seem as important as having sex. When we got off the phone, I went to listen to that Morrissey song "We Hate It When Our Friends Become Successful." They understood jealousy in the early nineties. Then I went and called Goose and asked him when he was coming for that visit.

PAGEANT WEAR

January 23
Today I found my Miss Smithers fashions. I set out intending to spend the Rod & Gunners' money with

care. I went alone because my mother doesn't approve, plus she has terrible taste and is not to be trusted in a public shopping setting. On a mother-daughter shopping trip last fall she got into a brawl with my archenemy since first grade, Linda. And when I say brawl, I'm not talking about pointed name-calling or a dainty slap or two. I mean actual punches flying and the two of them rolling around on the ground like the world's most pathetic WWF match. Needless to say, it was an extremely scarring experience that Death Lord Bob and I are still trying to work through.

I went to both of the main stores in town—Northlight Jeans and Herringbone & Heather. Their clothes were okay, hip and tasteful respectively, but I guess my eye is too accustomed to thrift stores. I saw nothing distinctive enough for the kind of candidate I plan to be.

But on my way home I went past Rotten Ryders, the biker shop. They had a couple of T-shirts in the window, and on a whim I went inside.

Now *they* had some distinctive clothes! Not to mention their staff.

The lady behind the counter had fright-wig blond hair, a Harley T-shirt, and jeans with zippers running up and down the length of both legs and right through the middle, so they would split into four pieces if fully unzipped. They were cool. She also had on a leather jacket with multiple fringes. Double cool.

"Yeah?" she demanded.

The place smelled of oil and leather. I could hear motorcycles revving and tools clanking in the shop out back.

"I'm shopping."

Frizz stared at me through a mask of black eyeliner.

"Ah, um. I'm looking for clothes."

Her scowl didn't move.

"I need something for this, you know, contest."

She dragged powerfully on her cigarette, and when she finally exhaled, only the barest wisp of smoke leaked out.

"What kinda contest?" she asked, and a few more tendrils of smoke snuck from her mouth.

"The Miss Smithers."

Her face stayed in position, but it's possible that a corner of her mouth cracked upward a fraction.

"Miss Smithers," she repeated. "No shit. Well, whaddya looking for? We ain't got no dresses in here."

Her arm fringes swept magnificently through the air and made a whooshing sound as she gestured around the shop to show me how frock-free it was.

"Oh, you know, something, um, distinctive. Special," I told her.

"Christ," she snorted. "Kids. I got a goddamn kid and she's fulla the goddamnedest ideas too. Last time we went to Vancouver, she wanted me to take her to Laura Friggin' Ashley. Hey Mick!" she yelled. "We got a clothes customer here."

When Mick didn't appear, she got up. The two-foot length of chain that ran from her belt loop into her pocket, reaching almost to her knee, clanked and jangled impressively as she stomped into the back.

"Mick!" she bellowed.

A biker appeared, wiping his hands on a dirty hand-kerchief. He was just like a regular biker, only smaller. His leather jacket was decorated with gang patches, and his dirty jeans sat low enough to give his belly room to move. He had long hair and a mustache, and besides the one in his hands, an assortment of kerchiefs sprouted here and there about his person. I imagine these were probably used for cleaning motorcycle parts, wiping sweat, gagging victims, and possibly disguising his face during armed robbery.

"Where the hell ya been?" demanded Frizz, who towered over Mick by a generous foot.

Mick didn't reply as he finished wiping his hands on his kerchief.

Frizz turned to me.

"Mick here'll look after ya. He handles the duds. I only look after the bike parts."

With that she sat down at the counter, lit another cigarette, set it carefully in a tin ashtray to her left, deliberately placed her hands flat in front of her, and leaned forward to watch the transaction.

I got the feeling that her presence made Mick nervous, because he kept his eyes on the floor and his voice low.

He mumbled something I couldn't hear. Frizz couldn't hear it either.

"Whaddya think, she's a goddamn German shepherd? Who the hell can hear ya when ya talk so low? Kid wants somethin' distinct like. Unusual."

Mick made a throat-clearing noise like he was thinking and walked over to a rack. He held up a giant Harley Davidson T-shirt.

I shook my head.

Frizz snorted. "Distinct goddamn! That's about as distinct as a friggin' ball bearing."

. He growled again and pointed to a row of leather jackets hanging on the wall.

I shook my head with the smallest movement I could make, afraid to offend Frizz by rejecting something she had on. But she agreed.

"She's in the Miss Smithers, Mick, for Chrissakes, not the biker groupie contest. Jesus, use yer head."

Finally Mick turned to a rack of chaps and leather pants. Frizz dismissed the chaps, telling him I wasn't no S&M cowboy. But at the pants she paused.

"Them ain't bad. Not indecent or nothin'. Good quality. Try 'em on, kid."

So I did. Using the oil storage cupboard in the corner, I struggled into the biker pants. They weighed approximately fifty pounds, and the moment I put them on, I knew I had to have them.

I stepped out of the cupboard to show Frizz and Mick. Frizz raised her eyebrows and gave a long low whistle.

"Not bad."

Mick nodded seriously.

Frizz made me turn this way and that, and she nodded her approval at each new perspective.

"Not bad. Not too damn bad."

One of the mechanics emerged from the back.

"Hey Dirty, whaddya thinka these, eh?" Frizz asked him.

I nearly died, but Dirty was respectful.

"Nice."

"Yeah," she agreed. "Mick picked 'em out. He's got a eye for clothes, I always said."

Mick rubbed a kerchief over his face.

She turned back to me. "Now obviously these ain't for the big night or nothin'. They're more of your daytime-casual-typa wear. Ain't no other girls gonna have a paira these. That's for goddamn certain."

Maybe it wasn't the best idea in the world to spend all but $30 of my $400 clothing allowance on one pair of pants, but I considered myself lucky to get them for that.

Frizz gave me a 15 percent discount "On accounta you bein' a candidate and all." Which might be illegal, Rotten Ryders most likely being a criminal organization. But I didn't care.

"If ya win, kid, maybe in yer speech you could mention Rotten Ryders and how Mick helped ya out, eh?"

I assured her I would. It's amazing what leather pants can do for a person's confidence and individuality. Let's see the other candidates come up with pageant wear that can compete with leather pants! I'm so excited, I feel ready to crack open one of my birthday notebooks and write my first 'zine article.

Later

Here it is. My first offering as a journalist. I'm not sure, but I think it may even have a bit of a poetic quality due to the depth of feeling.

Rotten Ryders:
Not All That Rotten Really

You've probably passed by the shop a million times and thought, "I'd never go in there. That place is full of criminals and people who hardly ever take baths." And while it is true that the Rotten's

staff have a different sense of
style than you see down at Herringbone & Heather, it is also
true that there is room for more
leather in this town.

If you decide to check out Rotten's, go prepared for swearing.
You will also be excited to learn
that they offer the services of an
on-site fashion consultant, who
is not tall but seems pretty good
at following directions.

Did I buy anything? That's my
little secret. But just between
you and me, let's say that nothing feels quite like leather
against bare skin.

—Alice MacLeod,
a.k.a. P. J. Hervey

The article's so good, I'm tempted to use my real
name. After all, P. J. Harvey is already known to be
talented. I, on the other hand, am not. Maybe I could

make my byline "Alice MacLeod writing as P. J. Hervey"? I suppose that kind of defeats the purpose of a *nom de pen*.

Now I just have to decide what to do with my 'zine once I've got a few articles together. Obviously, I need to publish it, but maybe not around here, as there may be incriminating material in it. And I need to come up with a gimmick, like printing it on the backs of envelopes or something. 'Zines are expected to look different because they are considered an alternative form of media.

Whew! I've really got a lot on my plate. It seems like just last week I was two people away from friendless and a virgin. Well, I guess I'm still that, but now I'm also a journalist and a candidate.

Unfortunately, the expense of my leather pants has forced me to economize on the rest of my Miss Smithers wear. It took me fifteen minutes of hard digging in the Seniors Bin at the New on You United Church Secondhand Store to come up with a two-piece purple suit that more or less fits me. The shoulder pads are admittedly a bit extreme and the ruffle on the bias-cut skirt has seen better days, but the thick gold chain belt fits just right. It is my hope that people will take the suit for early-eighties hipness on my part, rather than an artifact originally belonging to someone who was already old in the 1960s.

A 'ZINE BY ANY OTHER NAME

January 25
George called. She's not coming to visit in two weeks like she was supposed to. She's going to another 4-H rally. She's all worked up because that boy she did IT with will be there. I listened very politely and didn't get upset or annoyed. Really, as a writer and a candidate, I am busy and have other things on my mind besides whether George is going to keep her commitments. Like the fact that Goose is coming to visit in a few days to help me put out my 'zine—and, unbeknownst to him, I've decided he's going to assist me in my march toward sexual experience. George was too self-involved to ask how I'm doing, or, more specifically, if I have any sex-related news to report, and I am too self-reliant to tell her. But soon she won't have anything on me. I'll have had sex *and* I'll be a candidate.

Later

Like Charles Dickens and Tolstoy before him, both of whom were also quite proletariat, I write a lot. Today I wrote several articles, some of which I include here because they are really good.

It's Not Who Does It First

Some people, particularly teenage people, take pride in being the first of their friends to have sex.

Those people are misguided.

Sex is a serious matter. A person shouldn't have sex until they are old enough and mature enough to deal with the consequences. Which can be severe.

In the final reckoning, the person who has sex with someone they love is probably the winner over someone who makes it with someone they barely know. If you are having sex and think that makes you more advanced than your

friends who aren't doing it yet,
think again. Maybe that friend of
yours has better things to do.
Maybe he or she is active in the
community, for instance.

In closing, just remember that
just because someone hasn't had
sex yet, doesn't mean she hasn't
tried.

Think about it.

—P. J. Hervey

That one may need a bit of work. But the next
one is excellent.

What Is the Miss Smithers
Pageant and Why Does it Matter?

We all think we know what a beauty
pageant is. It's beautiful girls
with a lot of talent who are also
very nice.

Well, our homegrown version of
a beauty pageant is something else

again. It appears to be a platform for local businesses to sponsor candidates and events in an effort to raise their own profile. But, unfortunately for whoever thought up this scheme, the quality of the contest is compromised by the small population base the pageant has to draw from, which is no one's fault and can't be helped.

But here's another thing. According to the dictionary, a pageant is supposed to be a "brilliant spectacle." According to one source close to the action, the pageant is in danger of becoming a spectacle of cattiness and tight jeans if some of the candidates (are you listening, Miss Main Street?) don't watch their tendency to be mean to others. The contestants need to live up to the spirit of the pageant as spectacle and try a little harder to be

all they can be, lookswise and
heartwise.

The town of Smithers deserves
it.

—P. J. Hervey
[a.k.a. Alice MacLeod]

Don't ask me why that article is so pro-Smithers. It just seems that if you're going to write an article criticizing something, you have to find something else to be positive about. I actually think that Smithers and all the sponsors deserve the lousy candidates they get. This town breeds bad behavior, and people like me pay the price. But that doesn't exactly sound like journalistic integrity and distance, does it? Which reminds me that if I'm going to be ruthlessly honest in my 'zine, I better make sure no one finds out who wrote it. I'd hate the pageant organizers and judges to get wind of the fact that they've got a Ted Conover-type journalist in their midst. Although, truth be told, my cutting-edge sense of style probably gives it away.

FACE FRONT AND SMILE

January 28

We made an all-candidates trip to the *Interior News* office after school today to give the reporter our bios and have our photos taken. Several of the girls went all out and had their hair and makeup professionally done. They denied it when asked by the others, but the change in their appearance was too extreme to attribute to regular grooming.

I spent the event speculating on who among my fellow candidates has had sex.

Miss Bulkley Valley Fall Fair, who has long, straight hair, arrived with a full head of tight curls and a faceful of pancake makeup. I'd call her a maybe. Miss Main Street had on so much blue eye shadow and blue mascara, it was a wonder she could keep her eyes open. She's an obvious sex haver from way back.

When Miss Forest Products (a very likely), who was pretending to be *au natural* but was actually just hiding behind several layers of sheer makeup in natural colors, asked Miss Fall Fair why she had on so much makeup, Miss Fall Fair snarled that everyone knows you have to go dramatic for a black-and-white photo. Miss Evelyn Station Fish Hatchery nodded her agreement from behind a motionless mask of orange foundation and a cloud of hair-product fumes. (I'd have to put her down for carnal knowlege.)

The other candidates were all convinced that my noneffort at looking good was just an affectation to make them feel bad about their own beauty machinations. When I told them that I just forgot about pictures today, Miss Frontage Road (unlikely, due to her affection for that hideous lime-green sweater that she was wearing again today) snorted and whispered, "Yeah, right," to Miss Main Street. I wasn't about to tell them that I'm preoccupied about the imminent loss of my virginity when Goose gets here this weekend, although my casual observations suggest that quite a few of them could relate.

I almost didn't make it to the shoot at all. Finn called me at four o'clock to ask me what I was wearing for the photos. I had to race out the door to make it to the newspaper offices in time. I didn't get a chance to change out of my Roxy Music T-shirt, the one with the spaghetti stains all over the front, or fix my hair, so

I kept my toque and parka on. I must have looked like a criminal, especially since the photographer just lined us up against the wall like he was taking mug shots.

The photos will be in the newspaper in a few days. I am actually quite excited.

On another note, it looks like we've already lost one candidate. Miss Unschooling didn't show up for the pictures. But Miss Deschooling did, and she's demonstrating signs of a backbone. She wore a light blusher. One girl down, thirteen to go before I have a chance at winning the pageant!

The only damper is that I heard Miss Panelboard Plant (probably) inviting a few of the other candidates to go out for a nonofficial "just us girls" dinner next week. She didn't invite me. I bet I'm the only one who wasn't invited. I am accustomed to ostracism, but I thought things would be different once I was a candidate. That hurt. What is it about me that signals to groups of girls that I should be shunned and tormented? Because I am a Conoverian-type serious journalist, I didn't let my feelings interfere with my most recent work, a Miss Smithers score chart.

My chart is probably going to bring this contest the kind of attention it's always needed. In the past, everyone in town basically ignored the pageant unless they or a close relative were in it. But now, with my score chart, everyone will be able to track the progress of the candidates. It may even get some interest from local gambling addicts.

Keeping everyone's score similar was quite diplomatic of me. The low scores I gave myself were a particularly nice, humble touch. It's enough to make me want to bump up my congeniality scores.

Deep Inside Miss Smithers:
Part I

The preliminary results for the Miss Smithers Pageant are in! Even before the judging starts! An inside source has revealed the standings thus far! (Please note that these scores are out of a possible ten and are not guaranteed to be scientific.)

Come on, girls! You're going to have to work a little harder to improve those scores!

—P. J. Hervey

COMPETITOR	BEAUTY	TALENT	CONGE-NIALITY	FASHION SENSE	COMMENTS
Miss 4-H	3	3	3	3	Candidate stands out as having healthy lifestyle. More attention could be paid to developing feminine traits. A bit more biceps disguise might be in order.
Miss Northern Real Estate	3	NSF (none so far)	NSF	3	Candidate narrowed eyes and hissed "shut up" when asked about unfair advantage. But was wearing nice shoes.
Miss Main Street	NSF	NSF	NSF	NSF	Candidate's pants were tight. Hair was large. Needs a lot of work to make it onto chart in any capacity.
Miss Panelboard Plant	3	3	NSF	3	Contestant made other contestants feel left out. Contestant has permanently blown her chance to get on the chart for congeniality. Obviously doesn't know the meaning of a pageant.
Miss Unschooling	3	3	3	3	Candidate seems vulnerable. An early casualty?

COMPETITOR	BEAUTY	TALENT	CONGE-NIALITY	FASHION SENSE	COMMENTS
Miss Deschooling	3	3	4	2	Candidate is at least braver than her Unschooling counterpart. Use of makeup shows promise.
Miss Loggers' Association	NSF	NSF	5	3	Candidate is at least friendly, which may be linked to the smell of alcohol on her breath. Inebriated condition leads to some interesting fashion choices.
Miss Ski Smithers	7	7	7	7	Candidate is almost perfect. Will she peak too early?
Miss Forest Products	3	3	3	3	Candidate needs to work on distinguishing herself from the many other tree-related contestants.
Miss Frontage Road	NSF	NSF	NSF	NSF	Should be told that lime-green sweater makes her look like Cold Case File from *Investigative Reports*. Should also be informed about the number of muscles required for smiling versus frowning.

COMPETITOR	BEAUTY	TALENT	CONGE- NIALITY	FASHION SENSE	COMMENTS
Miss Evelyn Station Fish Hatchery	3	3	3	3	Needs to work on something other than application of eye makeup. Multiple small braids should be rethought.
Miss Chicken Creek Fire Department	3	3	3	3	Seems a decent person. Too bad about sponsoring organization's name.
Miss Bulkley Valley Fall Fair	3	NSF	1	3	Being overambitious is never attractive. Needs to spend less time trying to make others look bad while making self look good.
Miss Rod & Gun Club	3	3	NSF	3	Is rumored to be a good writer.
Miss Moricetown	3	3	NSF	3	Very fit, but do politics have a place in a beauty pageant? If so, she's got a real shot.

KAREN FIELD: TEEN QUEEN

February 1

I was at Van's News this morning when it opened. There we were, all fifteen of us in black and white. The photos were amazing! Even I looked pretty good in a ghostly, overdressed sort of way.

While I was buying my copy of the paper, Miss Frontage Road came in, still sporting her lime-green sweater. She may have more than one of them. When she saw me, she frowned and said, "Just getting some gum."

Yeah, right.

Later

Life isn't all beauty pageants. There's still school to endure. I'm enrolled in typing at the regular school this term. I was going to drop it, but now that I'm a journalist, I've decided to take it more seriously. Apparently real reporters can type something like thirty words a minute or even more, so I have my work cut out for me.

I sat down and was all set to really apply myself when the girl next to me nodded a greeting and looked at me over her wire-rimmed glasses. I nearly fell out of my chair, because it wasn't just any girl, it was Karen Field, party girl—smoking-area elite. She'd never noticed me before. I am one of the weirdos from the Alternative. Karen Field is normal school royalty! She smokes, drinks, wears womanly clothes such as halter tops and dress slacks and high-heeled boots, dates older men, *and* gets straight As. She's always surrounded by her gang of popular girl clones. None of them know I'm alive, and the fact that their queen noticed me nearly sent me into cardiac arrest.

I nodded back and tried not to stare at her hair. Karen's hair had the kind of reckless unmoving perfection that only hours of labor and half a bottle of Joico Ice Mist could achieve: sort of how Medusa would look if she got a job as a hair model. The wild snaking mass of curls glimmered with highlights in three or four complementary yet contrasting shades.

Karen Field had knife-sharp creases in her jeans, and her short velvet jacket looked like a recently vacuumed shag rug. Her makeup glowed fresh under the fluorescent lights, and her fingernails ended in little white half moons. She looked a well-preserved twenty-five if she looked a day. If anyone should have been a candidate for Miss Smithers, it was Karen. But truly cool girls never run for Miss Smithers. They don't have to win some contest to prove they rule. And here the queen of them all had just acknowledged me. I must be getting cooler!

While the rest of the class practiced keyboarding exercises, Karen's gang curled their hair with their portable curling irons, fixed up their makeup, and drank coffee. A couple of them slept, heads on desks, giant hair ruffling in the vented breeze.

Karen had a book propped open in front of her keyboard and was shaping her nails with an emery board as she read.

"How's it going?" she asked.

I tried not to gush when I responded.

"Oh, hi. Hi!"

"I saw your picture in the paper this morning."

"Really?"

"Good shot of you. Black and whites are the best, eh?"

"Yeah." I nodded, a little too vigorously.

"The hat was a cool touch. Like you didn't care."

Oh my God. Karen Field liked my hat.

"Yeah. I, uh, hope so. You know."

Encouraged by Karen's endorsement, I really threw myself into the first few minutes of keyboarding: acacac ddd adadadada ppp.

When my fingers got tired, I stopped and shook out my hands, convinced that in another five minutes I'd have a full-blown case of carpal tunnel syndrome.

"You've got to stretch them."

This from Karen, who still hadn't looked up from her book.

I pulled on my fingers a bit. Karen let her glasses fall down her nose and peered over at me.

"Like this."

She spread her fingers wide and then scrunched them into fists.

I copied her as exactly as I could, trying not to let my eyes veer off onto her hair.

The teacher came around, gripping a huge mug of coffee.

"I trust we're keyboarding here, ladies?"

I nodded and went back to my two-finger tap-tapping. Karen began typing at a phenomenal speed.

She must've been typing at least ninety words a minute. Unreal. The teacher nodded with satisfaction. As soon as she'd moved on, Karen stopped keyboarding and started reading again.

"I figure I'll get more out of reading Maugham than typing him," she said, and was lost to the world again.

No wonder Karen runs the smoking area.

Later

At my counseling session I discovered that Bob has hung up my pageant portrait from the newspaper in his office. I know I'm his only successful client, but that seems almost like playing favorites. What are the other troubled teens going to think? I feel like the Troubled Teen of the Month at the Teens in Transition (Not in Trouble) Center. I hope Bob isn't getting his hopes up too high. I mean, my winning isn't exactly a foregone conclusion. At least not yet.

Bob picked up on my nervousness about Goose's visit, which is due to start in a few hours and may end with me becoming a woman in the carnal knowledge sense. Bob's not bad on the early detection, but he lacks follow-through.

"I can see you're nervous about something," he

said in his most insightful voice, as though noticing that I was pacing around and eyeing the clock required the skills of Sherlock Holmes, Freud, and the entire cast of *Law and Order* combined.

"Yeah, you know," I said.

For a moment I thought that it might be good to talk the whole sex-having plan over with Bob. But he didn't dig any deeper.

"The pageant, right?" he said with a self-satisfied air. "I get it. I really do. But don't worry. You'll do great. *We'll* do great. And if you need any help with the public speaking part, you just let me know."

Bob really is hopeless sometimes.

So as usual, I'm on my own with this decision. To do it or not to do it. That is the question.

IN THE FACE OF ADVERSITY

February 6

Goose left school early and arrived at three o'clock yesterday, right on time, but that was the only thing that went right on my Loss of Virginity Weekend. My plan was to have sex almost immediately so my parents wouldn't have a chance to get in the way. Then Goose and I would put together my 'zine.

When I opened the door, Goose stood on the porch, grinning, his hands full of bits of metal and plastic.

"Lost a few pieces of the truck on the way here," he said. "Had to keep stopping to pick them up."

He looked fantastic. That tingle I get whenever I see him traveled down my spine and landed somewhere deep. He reached to hug me, forgetting that his hands were full, and dropped everything. The truck parts clattered all over the porch and down the stairs. I watched him on his hands and knees, scrambling for strays, and I had a flash of misgiving. He reached for a tube-shaped piece and knocked it with his hand so it shot out onto the walkway. My misgivings grew. That automotive part could be me!

Goose finally stood up, still smiling, with his hurricane hair and a smear of grease across his cheek.

"Got it!" He brandished the piece of pipe at me. "Dented but not broken!"

My deep feeling sputtered back to life.

"Daniel!" My parents were on us, pushing me out of the way in their enthusiasm to welcome Goose, son of Ph.D.s, into our home. It was as though my mother had never interrupted Goose and me *in fragrante* at the Terrace Community Center last fall.

"How are you, Dan?" My dad ushered Goose into the kitchen.

"And how are your parents?" my mother asked, getting right to the point. "And your brother's doctoral work? How's that going?"

My mother loves mentioning the doctoral work and does so in nearly every sentence she speaks to Goose.

"I hear doctoral work is very challenging," she'll say, passing the miso gravy, or "that's the way with doctoral work," in the middle of a conversation about Goose's twelfth-grade history class.

My mother is so excruciating.

We had an early dinner, which was a full-on lentil loaf feast during which my mother asked about Goose's parents' doctoral work about fifty times. I found myself looking at him and feeling torn between attraction and anxiety. Did George have any fear before she did it? Maybe it would be simpler with someone you didn't know that well. The whole thing just seemed so invasive.

As we were leaving the table, Goose asked to see MacGregor's aquariums, which was all the confirmation I needed that Goose was the right man for the job, so to speak. MacGregor happily showed Goose his tanks and explained his guppy experiment, which aquarists all over the world are apparently following with great interest on the Internet. Then Goose tripped on his way out of the room, and barely missed ruining the science project under construction on Mac's desk. If Goose'd landed a few inches to the right, there would have been toothpicks, Popsicle sticks, and carpenter ants as far as the eye could see.

"Are you okay?" asked Mac, who is a very thoughtful person.

"Sure. No problem," said Goose.

When I finally got Goose into my room, I left my door open to avoid parental suspicion. He asked me to tell him all about the pageant. Then we looked at the newspaper photos. He said that I was the cutest by far, even though it wasn't true. Then he asked to see the clothes I'd bought. I was so thrilled to show someone! I changed in the closet for privacy's sake, which was difficult because it's not exactly a walk-in or anything. Goose waited on the bed. He was so nice and complimentary about the purple old-person's suit that by the time I got in the closet to put on the *piece of resistance*, my leather pants, I knew it was nearly time to go ahead with the life-changing experience. I was ready.

When I stepped out of the closet wearing my stiff new pants, his eyes shot open and his blond hair seemed to stick up even higher.

I moved toward him and he stood to meet me. We were practically drowning in each other's eyes. He reached over and swung shut my bedroom door in this very manly way. And suddenly we were making out, falling onto my bed with what I guess you would call sheer passion.

I was ready. It was time. I couldn't think. We were both sort of panting and kissing and I was in leather pants and the whole thing was just unbelievably sexy. In a minute, we'd be actually doing it.

Then, without warning, he stopped, slid out from under me, and lay there with a hand over his chest as though he was having a heart attack. I was left, face-planted in my bed, sweating in my leather pants.

"Oh man," he said.

I pushed myself up onto my elbows, arms weak. "What?"

He didn't answer.

"What?" I asked again.

"Your parents. They just gave me dinner. And your pants. Oh my God. Your pants."

"My parents don't care. What about my pants? Don't you like them?"

"I *love* your pants. I love them too much."

"So what's the problem?" I demanded.

He just shook his head.

"I'm sorry. I just can't."

I grabbed my pillow, held it to my face, and yelled.

Telling myself I would never allow my parents to be nice to another boyfriend, I changed into clothes that Goose could handle. I was furious but not sure why. I felt like he led me on, showing up here in his old jeans, underwear poking out, not intentionally like on a Calvin Klein model but because it is pulled up too high. It was a come-on, and it made me mad. Goose was clumsy. He got me going and then he dropped me. Or maybe not. All I knew is I was steamed.

I got out my 'zine notebook and handed it to him.

"Here."

He looked startled.

"You're going to have to use the typewriter.

Printer's broken," I directed him. "Go ask Mac or my mom or dad to show you where it is."

He looked taken aback. "Oh, okay. Well, I guess I'll type it?"

"Whatever."

He cleared his throat nervously and continued.

"So we'll, I mean, I'll type it up. And then we can photocopy it or something." He looked over for some sign of agreement.

I shrugged and then stared up at the ceiling. He was silent for a while, and I snuck a glance at him. He'd opened the bedroom door again and was sitting on the floor, his back against the bed, reading the notebook.

I went back to thinking unclean thoughts.

My parents looked in on us several times, smiling, wrinkling their noses and crinkling their eyes. Each time they passed, Goose waved vigorously at them. I realized that we'd never have gotten away with keeping the door shut for long enough to have sex. Somehow that made me even madder. Maybe he should be my parents' boyfriend.

Finally, he closed the notebook.

"This is good. Interesting. But are you sure you want people to, um, read it?"

I turned my head and gave him the thousand-yard stare from a distance of three feet.

"Why wouldn't I?"

He cleared his throat again. "It's just that if, well, if people in the pageant read it—"

"What?"

"It's just that . . . oh nothing."

"I don't care what people think. It's all true."

"Okay. So I'll go type this up?"

Again, no answer from the Queen of the Sullen People.

Goose turned at the doorway.

"I'm sorry, Alice. It's not that I don't want to. You know I do. But right after dinner with your parents in the next room might not be the best time. Maybe it's a cliché, but it should be special. Or at least uninterrupted."

Over the next couple of hours I could hear him talking to my parents and MacGregor. I blamed him for that too, even though he was acting under my direction. He came back periodically to report his progress.

"It's going well."

"I'm almost done typing."

"That's a crazy old typewriter your dad has. No correction tape."

Then, "Want to come down to the photocopy place? Your mom said she'd drive us on her way back from the library. She wants to get there before it closes at nine."

I was in the record-breaking sulk of a lifetime. I couldn't be interrupted. How many opportunities was I going to get to be this hard done by? This wronged? I was a master of silent scorn. Nobody messes with a Miss Smithers candidate and escapes unscathed!

"Come on, Alice," he tried again, then sighed and gave up.

"We'll be back soon."

By the time Goose and my mom returned, I didn't have the strength for another Olympic-caliber performance in the Most Angry Event for Girls 17 and Under. Frosty was the best I could do.

Goose came into my room and dropped a stack of photocopies on the bed. "Here they are."

"Hmmm."

"Oh come on. Don't you want to look? They're excellent."

I glanced at them. "They're green."

"It was the cheapest paper. It's kind of eye-catching, I think. I paid for them myself," he added.

"I'll pay you back."

In a supremely selfless gesture, he said, "That's okay. You don't have to."

Poor Goose. He was trying so hard. He was wearing a nice shirt. I could just see him finding his nice shirt and putting it on and driving here, so hopeful and everything.

My parents poked their heads into my room.

"You feeling better, honey?"

"Yeah. A bit." I looked at Goose and he nodded.

"Why don't you two come play Monopoly? It's better with more people."

I was about to say no, but Goose was on his feet, nodding, hands in his wrinkled stretched-out pockets, toes poking through his threadbare brown socks, eager to please. I sighed and said, "Oh, all right."

I figured I owed him that at least.

By midnight I had every property from Pennsylvania to Kentucky, and a stranglehold on the railways. Goose, bankrupt, was eating rice treats and advising MacGregor, who had hotels on the Connecticut strip but poor cash flow. My dad was on his last legs, financially speaking, and my mom was mortgaged to the hilt. To take her mind off her approaching insolvency, she changed the subject.

"So—where are you going to put your newspaper?" she asked me.

"It's a 'zine. Pay me my money. Keep your mind on the game."

She handed over the money for Short Line.

"I dropped a few of your newspapers at the library when I took back our books. Including some books I found buried in your room yesterday, Miss."

Goose and I spoke together. "You what?"

"I knew the librarian would like to see it."

"But I haven't even looked at it yet," I said, then added, "And what were you doing in my room?"

She was breezy. "I'm sure it's fine, Alice. It's only a couple of pages. I thought I'd help you out by tidying up before Daniel arrived. He's probably used to a certain level of order. His parents are scientists."

"But Mom, you can't just give my 'zine to anyone you want. And since when do you clean anything?"

"It'll be fine, honey. It's great that you are doing something so creative. And don't be rude. I do so clean."

"Come on, Alice," said my dad, who had a measly house each on Park Place and Boardwalk. "Come on. Enough of the housekeeping debate. Roll the dice. You're headed for the high-rent district now. This is where your luck changes!"

Of course, I didn't land on either of his properties. I just breezed past Go and collected my $200. It wasn't until the next morning that I realized my dad was right. My luck had changed.

During the night nothing happened between Goose and me. He's no George's boyfriend. He didn't come sneaking out of the guest room into my room with a condom in his pocket and a rose in his teeth. And when he came upstairs in the morning, I was not in the mood.

"You left my name on some of the articles."

"I typed what I saw."

"But I crossed it out."

"Not everywhere you didn't, or I wouldn't have typed it."

"You didn't think, 'Gee, maybe she doesn't care about publishing this because she's written it under a false name?'"

"You said you didn't care who read it."

"That's because no one was supposed to know it was me. How could you let my mom put them in the library? My life is ruined."

"Your life is not ruined. I'm sorry, I didn't notice. I stayed in the car when she went in. I didn't see her take them. We'll just go get the ones your mom left at the library. No one is going to read it."

This was a disaster. Sexual frustration collided with fear of humiliation, making me feel like I was about to explode. I put my head in my hands and moaned.

Goose tried to reason with me.

"You wouldn't talk to me last night. How was I supposed to know what you wanted?"

"It should have been obvious."

He just looked at me. "I can't believe–"

"You can't believe what?"

He shook his head. "Come on. Let's just go to the library."

Later

The librarian, Mrs. Davis, played dumb. When she finally opened the doors and let us in at ten, after we'd been waiting outside not speaking for an hour, I asked her if my mother'd accidentally returned some photocopies with our library books.

"Your name?"

"Alice. Alice MacLeod."

"Hmm. Let's just have a look."

She typed my name into her computer and said, "Aha. Alice MacLeod. Right. You know you have a late charge, don't you?"

"Oh really? I didn't know. I was just looking for, like, these, um, photocopied 'zines actually, that I left here. Or my mother did. I just need them back. They aren't finished. They aren't really library-type items even. . . ."

She ignored me.

"Yes, it says here that *Cat in the Hat* was almost nine years overdue. And *Black Beauty*: seven years overdue."

She peered over her bifocals at me. "If we charged you full rate, your library fines would be rather impressive, Ms. MacLeod. They'd come to a total of three hundred dollars. As it is you'll have to pay at least replacement value on those items."

"Oh man. Well, I don't really know about that. I mean, those books, they must have been lost. And you did get them back. I was more interested in getting back the photocopies that my mother accidentally–"

She pursed her lips and shook her head.

"We don't have anything like that."

"But you haven't looked."

"We don't have them. Do come and see us when you'd like to pay your fines. And say hello to your brother for me. He's always so good about returning his books."

And that was it. Stonewalled and hung out to dry by a librarian. It's like being bitten by a seeing-eye dog. It's not supposed to happen.

Goose tried to convince me that it wasn't the end of the world. He said that as a librarian, she would be a woman of her word.

"Then why wouldn't she give them back to me?"

"Maybe the janitor recycled them."

"What if the janitor is some kind of pervert who likes reading the personal papers of young girls?"

"A 'zine isn't exactly personal. You were planning to publish it. Why else did we make all those copies?"

"Exactly. Why *did* you make all those copies?"

Goose looked at me. "Maybe because you told me to."

We walked in silence for a while.

He tried again. "Look, I'm really sorry. But you have to look at the situation."

I gave it some thought before I said it. But it wasn't a particularly thoughtful thought.

"You just can't get anything right, can you?"

We were standing in our driveway, and I could see his breath plume out of his mouth as I spoke.

"Seriously. You are totally hopeless and useless at everything, aren't you?"

His eyes, bright in the cold, looked at me.

"I'm going to go," he said. "Good luck with the pageant. And the writing and everything."

Regret hit me like a piano dropped from a tall building. I wasn't even angry really. Why did I have to be so awful to him? It was like I'd been testing my power and blown a fuse. Totally scorched the whole circuit.

I followed him into the house, where he went to get his things. My family was in the kitchen.

"Daniel. Alice. Where have you guys been? Can we get you something to eat?"

"That's okay, Mr. and Mrs. MacLeod."

"Please. Call us John and Diane."

"Thanks. I actually have to get going."

"But you just got here!" My mother sounded dismayed.

"Yeah, it's just that something came up at home. You know. But thanks for everything."

My parents looked at me, suspicion in their eyes. We all went outside to say good-bye.

"Drive safe, Dan!" said my father.

"Come back soon!" said my mother.

MacGregor just waved.

If they'd left us alone for ten seconds, I would have gone over and said I was sorry. I'd have told him that I didn't mean what I said. I'd have told him that I loved his imperfection and his honesty, the way he didn't pretend to be Mr. Got It All Together. I'd have told him that I liked his secondhand clothes and his do-it-yourself haircuts.

But I didn't say any of that. Because I am a coward. Plus my parents were hanging around as usual. This whole thing is practically their fault.

February 7

I've written Goose an apology. Because I'm a writer now, it's a better-than-average letter. I say sorry without really blaming myself. Reading it over, I'd have to say it's a win-win apology letter. He did wrong but it wasn't his fault. I was harmed but won't hold a grudge. They say that writing the hard-to-write letter is, well, hard. But for real writers, such as myself, it's not that difficult. I'm going to send the letter as soon as I'm sure the missing 'zines aren't going to ruin my life. Writing such an effective letter has really been a confidence booster. I was feeling quite depressed, but I'm coming out of it already. Goose is right. Those 'zines are probably in the shredder right now.

I may still be an unpublished virgin who recently and tragically lost her relationship due to a silly mix-up, whose future is mortgaged by extremely large library fines, and whose eventual triumph in the Miss Smithers Pageant is precarious at best, but things are looking up.

ABOUT MISS MAIN STREET'S SCORES . . .

February 8

Goose will not be receiving his apology letter anytime soon.

Any thought that my missing 'zines were sitting in a recycle box somewhere, safely unread, was exploded today at school. The other shoe dropped. And as usual, it dropped on me.

It was after lunch and I was on my way to the Alternative School portable building, home to the most maladjusted students of Smithers, B.C., of which I am a card-carrying member, when three of the toughest girls outside of professional wrestling intercepted me. They went to the regular school and were obviously upset about something. They didn't keep me in suspense.

"What's this you said about Miss Main Street in your little newspaper, you hose?"

"Answer us, weirdo."

"Yeah. Who do you think you are? She's my cousin, you know."

The sense of *déjà vu* was sickening. This was a replay of every other time I'd been physically menaced. My 'zine couldn't have fallen into worse, or larger, hands. Damn! I should have given Miss Main Street at least one positive score. But how? I'd have had to create a new category just for her: Cheap Looking with Big Hair.

They began to speak to each other rather than to me—never a good sign in my extensive experience of being victimized.

Head Bang One turned to Head Bang Two.

"Remember this girl?"

"No."

"Linda kicked her ass last fall."

"And she doctored up her bruises to make them look worse."

This was rich, and they all had a good cackle.

It's true I may have used a bit of makeup to accentuate the physical evidence after I was beaten up by the head tough girl of them all, Linda, a.k.a. the dread blond menace, my archenemy since first grade. But I'm theatrical by nature. You can tell from my writing.

I tried to make a move.

"Going somewhere, Writer Girl?" Head Bang Three, a bruise of a girl, moved between me and the safety of the building.

Why hadn't I enrolled in a self-defense course for the oddly dressed and misunderstood after the last attack? And why, oh why, hadn't I supervised Goose more closely when he did my work?

They all turned at once when a voice sounded behind them.

"Is this really necessary?"

I looked over expecting to see a teacher. But no. Behind us stood Karen Field, probably on her way to the regular school, perfect coiffure unmoving in the breeze.

Even the unsocialized Head Bangs One through Three weren't going to mess with Karen's pure popularity power, but that didn't stop them from grumbling a last warning before they slouched away.

"You're lucky, Hose Bag. You're just lucky Karen stepped in."

Head Bang Two had specific instructions.

"And my cousin better get mentioned in that newspaper of yours in the Pretty column or you're dead."

Karen didn't appear to notice them leaving. She was busy lighting a cigarette in blatant disregard of the fire hazard posed by the fumes coming off her head. Karen acted as though nothing had happened, as though she hadn't just saved me from yet another assault by Smithers Senior Secondary's Least Likely to Achieve set. She breathed a double jetstream of smoke straight into my face.

"I read your stuff," she said.

"Oh."

My mind raced. Had I written anything that was going to get me in trouble with the President of the Smoke Pit? Also, I was the only teenager I knew who went regularly to the library. How were all these people finding my 'zine? Someone must be distributing it.

"Yeah, it was pretty interesting," she continued.

"Interesting?"

"Your take on life . . . I liked it. That article about the leather. You're onto something there."

She exhaled another stream of smoke, and I caught an unmistakable scent of gin.

That Karen was truly sophisticated. She'd obviously been out for drinks at lunch.

"If you have any problems, let me know," she said finally, before going to join her teen posse, who stood smoking on the corner, waiting for her, poised, groomed, in their three-quarter-length belted jackets and high-heeled boots.

I am opposed to everything Karen and her friends stand for. Conformity, power, popularity. But I have to admit that I was sort of impressed. And grateful. Teachers and parents hadn't ever been able to protect me. All they'd done was sink me deeper into the mire of unpopularity and freakdom. But with Karen's seal of approval I would be untouchable, even with my 'zine making the rounds at Smithers Senior Secondary like an Oprah Book Club selection at the PTA.

Later I ran into Miss Bulkley Valley Fall Fair and cringed, expecting the worst.

"Hi." She smiled at me.

"Hi."

She'd never paid any attention to me before, much less talked to me. This was very suspicious.

"I totally think you should have been asked out for dinner with us. If it was up to me, you'd have been invited."

She was doing something odd with her lips, sort of pursing them while sucking in her cheeks. She was batting her eyes and angling her ear toward her shoulder. And she was wearing an exact replica of Miss Ski Smithers's dove-gray ensemble from the Meet the Queen night. She was posing! She was trying to get on the chart for congeniality and improve her beauty scores!

"So anytime you want to, you know, hang out. Maybe go shopping or something. That would be super."

"Right," I said. No way she was getting on the board through flattery.

There's power in this 'zine writing. Goose may get his apology after all.

Later

I wish I had someone to talk to about all that's going on, but I don't feel like calling George and hearing all about her sex life. And obviously I can't call Goose. At least not until I send the apology letter.

You'd think a counselor would fill the role of listener, but Bob is no regular counselor. My session with him this afternoon was—surprise, surprise—unfulfilling. Bob is getting careless through overconfidence, and I'm too sensitive and gentle to straighten him out.

"At least I don't have to worry about you," he said, working on replacing a screw in the cheap sunglasses he's begun wearing indoors, claiming snowblindness from a recent skiing trip. I'm sure the real reason he wears them is that he thinks they make him look like Lou Reed. I've read about the Velvet Underground in *Spin*. I know the look Bob's going for.

"Well..." I replied, giving him a clear opening to ask me how things are going. He's been my counselor for months now. You'd think he'd at least have that part down.

But no luck.

"Darn!" He dropped the tiny screwdriver.

"Sorry, I just have to grab this," he said as he disappeared behind his desk.

A card slid under the door, and I went and picked it up. "It's another Valentine's card for you."

"Oh thanks," he said from under his desk.

I added it to the stack on his desk. Bob's admirers were trying to get a jump on the rush by sending their declarations of love a few days early.

When he finally got his sunglasses fixed, he put them back on. They sat crooked on his face, two haphazard black circles. With his pointy black widow's peak and goatee he looked more like a badly drawn cartoon than a member of the Velvet Underground.

"So how's it going with the pageant? And your friends? Oh, is that another card? This is unbelievable, this outpouring. Such a friendly town," he said in his most sensitive voice, looking slightly embarrassed.

"It's fine," I said. "It's all fine."

Just when I think that man has made progress as a counselor, I realize we're a long way from finished.

In a disturbing side note, my Miss Smithers portrait from the newspaper has been joined by a picture of another Teen in Transition receiving a diploma for what was probably some very minor accomplishment. Obviously, I don't want to be counselor's pet or anything. But neither do I want to be just part of the riffraff.

On the plus side, at least Bob hasn't gotten hold of my 'zine yet.

Later

Thank goodness MacGregor was home working on his guppies this afternoon. He's a terrific listener. While he adjusted temperatures and made notes, moving from tank to tank inserting glass barriers between guppy couples and so forth, I lay on his neatly made bed and talked. I really got some things off my chest. Nothing too heavy out of respect for his youth. I just told him how disappointed and nervous I felt, how I blew it with Goose, and my worries about my leaked 'zine.

He listened, occasionally nodding or making a sympathetic gesture. He said he thought it might take people in the pageant a while to discover how interesting I was due to the sheer number of candidates. He said he hoped Goose and I worked it out because we were "nice together." About the 'zine he said, "It's probably so well-written, maybe it won't matter who wrote it." And he said all that while doing groundbreaking research into breeding guppies.

Before I got up to go, I remembered to ask, "How about you? How's it going?"

Mac smiled and nodded, using the end of his net as though using a cane to tip his hat to me. It was such an excellent gesture that I felt better for the rest of the night.

CROSSOVER HIT

February 14

You'd think that even if my leaked 'zine has damaged my prospects of fitting in within my own peer group, at least I'd be able to mix freely with aged people such as my parents and their friends. Think again.

Finn and Kelly and Marcus came over this afternoon. The three of them wore matching black I Love k.d. T-shirts. The T-shirts represented not Kraft Dinner, as Finn's unhealthy pallor might suggest, but k.d. lang, the singer. Finn's agenda was to get my parents to go with them to see another of his favorite performers, Ashley MacIsaac, the punk rock Celtic fiddler from Nova Scotia. Ashley was going to be in Prince George, which, at four hours away, is the closest city to Smithers, for a one-night-only performance.

"It's going to be the concert of a lifetime," Finn wheedled, knowing how much my dad dislikes leaving the house.

My dad, wearing his bathrobe and my mom's fuzzy slippers at four thirty in the afternoon, shrugged. "He's a fine musician, all right."

Kelly piped up, "They say he was a prodigy."

"Oh yes," gushed Finn. "You can't miss it. It'll remind you of your wasted youth—all the fans, all the acclaim," trying to tempt my dad with memories of his long-past glory days as a musician. "Even Marcus, that cretin, is going to come," he finished, disregarding Marcus, who sat directly to his left.

Finn's a big one for talking about people, even his best friends.

"Marcus is almost as culturally bankrupt as Kelly," he snorted, then noticed Kelly on his right. "Well sorry, but you're not exactly a season ticket holder at the opera, are you?"

Kelly didn't react. Nobody really listens to Finn's unpleasant remarks, because they usually don't make that much sense. Finn was on a roll now.

"Look, how many times do you think Ashley is going to be in Prince George? Once and never again! The only reason he's coming north at all is because his star's been dimmed by a passing cloud. It will rise and he'll never visit this backwater part of the world again!" Finn declared triumphantly.

My dad nodded in agreement, ready as always to be swayed by Finn's bad influence.

I had to ask. "You're going to see Ashley MacIsaac in Prince George? Can I go?" Ashley MacIsaac could be counted on for extreme and cutting-edge profanity, and I didn't want to miss that.

Finn declared imperiously, "Diane, tell the child that she's done enough!"

What was his problem? Wasn't he supposed to be my Miss Smithers mentor, my sponsor and guide? The competition was about to start heating up. I couldn't afford to lose a key member of my already meager support team at this early stage.

Finn leveled a gaze at me, raised an eyebrow, and said, "Well, I am so sorry if my clothes don't measure up to your standards. I can see that you're head-to-toe Versace yourself, eh? And your little notes on my personal relationships were also appreciated. A woman of the world such as yourself is in a real position to cast judgment on the ways of the heart."

Oh no. I'd forgotten the article about Finn. There were so many in the 'zine, it was hard to keep track of them all. I didn't think it was exactly bad. More unflattering, really. I walked with as much dignity as I could back to my room and read it.

It was bad.

Deep Inside Miss Smithers:
A Several Part Series:
The Mentors

Mentors matter.

That should be the motto of the Miss Smithers Pageant and the message for those ushering the candidates through this "life-changing experience."[1]

But as with the candidates themselves, there is room for improvement among the mentors. One, who shall remain nameless, is prone to criticizing his candidate's clothing sense, even though he himself is not exactly the last word in fashion. Someone, sometime, might consider telling him that just because an item of apparel is cheap, that doesn't mean it should be bought. For more information, please see <u>The Complete Guide to Thrifting: Cool versus Cheap and How to Spot the Difference</u>.

And another thing. The candidates are expected to reveal some sort of talent during the pageant. The same should be expected of the mentors. At risk of picking on one particular, nameless mentor, this reporter suggests that if we take him as an example, we can rule out the following activities: playing poker well, dressing well, and maintaining healthy relationships. What's left? Said individual and his friends have earned themselves the nickname the Geniuses, but unfortunately the term is used ironically.[2] This same individual has also perpetrated some of the most dysfunctional relationships[3] ever seen in this town, which is really saying something.

In conclusion, all the mentors, including the anonymous one mentioned in this article, need to work hard not to become liabilities in their candidates' campaigns.

—P. J. Hervey

[1] Outgoing Miss Smithers.
[2] It's sort of a long story. The mentor and his cronies play poker. One of the poker players' wives was embarrassed by this and told a friend they were having a men's meeting. The friend thought she said "Mensa Meeting." Now everyone in town is convinced the mentor and his three friends are much brighter than they look.

³ This individual's last boyfriend, a terminally ill man, was treated with reckless disregard by the mentor, due to being kind and gentle and having a healthy lifestyle. It is suspected that said mentor in question prefers romantic partners who a) have unhealthy lifestyles, b) are fundamentally negative in their attitudes toward life, and c) require no sympathy for serious illness. Not much of an example, is it?

Somehow Finn had gotten a copy of my 'zine. He didn't seem to appreciate the fact that I was being all David Foster Wallace with the footnotes. (D.F.W. is one of my favorite writers. When you're a writer yourself, you don't mind long, hard-to-understand books.) Finn should be proud that he was featured in the most modern and technically advanced article I've ever written. It must have been a lot of work for Goose to type up. It's interesting that my 'zine is penetrating the adult population. If I hadn't been in so much trouble, I would have been proud to have written what is shaping up to be a crossover success.

I went back into the kitchen. Finn started in on me as though I'd never left the room.

"And your clever little nicknames—I bet you think you're a bit of a genius yourself. Hmmm? A misunderstood genius, maybe? Well, young lady"— he was winding down now, attention span depleted—"it pays to be circumspect by word and by deed!" he finished, looking very proud of himself.

"Alice, you really should apologize to Finn if you wrote something rude about him in your newspaper," my dad said.

"'Zine," I corrected him.

"Oh, I can assure you that Alice should apologize to everyone in this room," Finn declared.

This was the big whatever. But I did want to go see the Piddler Fiddler, as my dad called Ashley MacIsaac when Finn wasn't around. Time to bring out the heavy artillery.

"Okay. Okay. I'm sorry that *someone* dropped off my private papers at the library without asking and that now my life is ruined." I managed to get my voice to crack slightly on the last word.

Then I swept out of the room.

That would teach Finn to try and discipline me. Nobody does teenage girl better than a teenage girl, not even Finn. They'll all feel so bad, they're sure to let me go to the concert now.

Did I mention that today was Valentine's? The less said about that, the better. My mom and dad gave me a card, which was almost worse than nothing. I nearly called Goose, but after Finn's visit I've lost the will to reach out. The writing life can be quite painful on holidays. On the plus side, at least I didn't get any bomb threats from disgruntled fellow candidates dissatisfied with my chart.

A VERY GOOD QUESTION

February 15
Fallout from publication continues. At lunch a long-haired guy came up to me where I was sitting alone, working on a 'zine article about how living in a valley surrounded by mountains can be psychologically oppressive and stop one from reaching one's full potential, or at least walking very far in any one direction. He invited me to a Young Christian Association meeting next week. The YCs are an impressive group in that they don't really mix much, and very little is known about them except that they are

nicer than average and less likely to get charged with impaired driving.

The long-haired guy said he understood that I was a "seeker" who might be interested in his organization's approach to chastity. My 'zine must be in its fourth printing by now! Is there anyone in this town who hasn't read it? He asked me to come out for an afterschool worship session.

"It'll be cool," he said.

I doubted that very much, but I said I'd go anyway. I couldn't help it. He was so attractive, I didn't really have a choice. In fact, I was surprised to find out he was religious. In spite of being kind and Christian and one of God's special children, Mr. Mother Teresa, whose real name is Mark, *looked* like he was on the other team. Sinful, in other words. He had smooth skin and piercing blue eyes. He wore a rawhide necklace with a fish hanging from it, sort of like the kind people stick on their cars. Only his was the sincere kind, not the ironic kind where the fish has legs or spells Darwin. In general, I prefer my men funny looking, but this guy was enough to make me reconsider.

He must've seen the confusion on my face, because he said, "What did you think? I was going to invite you to come out for the Young Socialists Society?" Then he laughed. "At our last prayer meeting we talked about your newspaper. I can't tell you how impressed we were. Especially with your stand on chastity. You're absolutely dead-on about that. There's no rush." He smiled perfectly at me. "We decided to give you this to help you on your path."

He held out a bracelet.

"Do you know what this is?"

"A bracelet?"

"You're terrific! No, seriously, it's a WWJD bracelet."

"Like WD-40?"

"That's great! No, but seriously. It's a reminder bracelet. WWJD stands for 'What Would Jesus Do?' Cool, eh?"

"Oh. Uh, yeah. I guess so."

"So whenever you're faced with a situation you don't know how to handle, the bracelet'll remind you to ask yourself what He would have done. It's sort of like having Jesus with you everywhere you go."

"On my wrist." I tried to hide the doubt in my voice.

"That's right. It's like having Jesus right on your wrist."

"Oh."

One little vote for not having sex and I become a takeover target for God himself. But what if Mark was just trying to get to know me? Like romantically. I *am* a Miss Smithers candidate, after all, and he just gave me jewelry.

"Excellent. So I hope we'll see you at the meeting next Monday. It's in Room Thirty-four, at three thirty. We'll have a good time. I know you'll like it."

"Great," I said, although it wasn't at all.

What Would Jesus Do? Holy crap, I have no idea. I'm the child of heathens. One thing I'm pretty sure Jesus would not do is notice that His would-be soul saver is hot.

I saw Miss Loggers' Association and Miss Frontage Road at school today. They both shot me dirty looks. But for once Miss Frontage Road wasn't wearing the hideous lime-green sweater, so in some sense I've done her a favor. Now that I've destroyed my chances for the congeniality award, it's a good thing I'm working on other areas, such as religious affiliation.

February 16
One benefit to attending the Alternative School is that they allow us some flexibility in our schedules.

About half the students attend only sporadically, which is why a lot of them have houses and kids but still haven't finished tenth grade. I probably have the fewest absentee days of anyone, so I didn't feel bad about staying home today. My parents know better than to force me. After all, I am a former home-schooled child and very independent minded.

I stayed home not because I was afraid of running into more angry candidates, but because I suspect that Jesus might have set the Alternative School on fire when faced with the magnitude of my sinning. I spent the day reading *The Mists of Avalon*, which is the closest thing we have to a religious book in our house. My parents are essentially heretics. Even Jesus wouldn't know what to do with them.

Later

I am crippled by Jesus. I can't do anything, I swear. There's nothing left for me but hanging out with prostitutes and the homeless. I've been looking into it in the family encyclopedia, and that's basically what Jesus did. Good thing He wasn't a sixteen-year-old living in Smithers, or He would've found life pretty tough.

I can't believe Christian Mark just dumped this bracelet on me with no preparation. I'm a strong person, but I wasn't prepared for this. God's only son on my wrist! How is a person supposed to function under this kind of pressure? It would be one thing if I had religious training. But I'm completely ignorant.

I went through all my activities and realized Jesus wouldn't have done even one of them. He wasn't worried about building a 'zine publishing career and He sure wasn't entering the Mr. Nazareth Pageant as Mr. God's Only Son. Blind ambition! That's all my life is.

I had grave doubts about going to my session today with Death Lord Bob. I seriously question whether Jesus would put His faith in Bob. But I figure God might cut me some slack for listening to such a godless person because a) I'm not His only son, and b) hanging with Bob is practically charity, since Bob's not what you'd call together. He's really sort of a prostitute of the mind, when you think about it. He'll counsel anyone for the right price. Jesus, on the other hand, had a specialized client base of the totally destitute, the physically disabled, and a few fallen women. He wasn't going around trying to drum up business among the lower middle classes the way Bob is. If Jesus went to Bob, it would be in the spirit of service and love.

With that in mind I went to my appointment early (practically unheard of) and actually *talked* to some of the other teens at the Teens in Transition (Not in Trouble) Center. If that doesn't put me on the fast track to salvation, I don't know what will.

"Hi," I said to the girl who looked most in need of spiritual assistance.

She ignored me, pulling her baseball cap down farther over her nose and slumping even lower in her chair.

"How are you today?" I asked in my most calming, Savior-like voice.

She didn't respond. Emma, a Teen Center regular notable for her Bible-story head of white curls, said: "I don't think Sadie's in the mood for socializing today. Would you like to play pin the tail on the character defect with me?"

I'd always avoided Emma before, sensing deep and numerous issues, but I looked down at my bracelet.

What would Jesus do?

"Uh, okay."

I hoped it was not a long game.

I sat down across from her and looked at the elaborate chart she'd drawn showing little stick figures arranged around a main stick figure topped with curly hair. She pointed at the curly stick girl.

"That's me."

She traced the jagged lines that ran from her stick figure out to the various other little stick people.

"And these are my broken and twisted relationships."

Then she held up several sheets of colored dot stickers—"And these are my character defects. Red is lust, yellow is fear, green is envy, and blue is overeating."

"Overeating is a defect of character?"

The ultrathin Emma casually withdrew a small pick from its hiding place in her cloud of hair and plucked out her curls a bit.

"Where I come from, overeating is a major sin! My sister"—she jabbed a finger at a particularly thin stick figure on her chart—"never overeats."

"So the sticker for her would be . . . ?"

She pursed her lips and stared at me.

"My problems with my sister are caused by *her* character defects! Self-righteous Pollyannaism, as indicated by the white stickers."

I saw then that the sister stick figure was nearly obliterated by a pox of white dots.

"There she is," said Emma, with extra venom, "my beauty-queen sister—Miss Ski Smithers."

Now this was interesting! Emma might be able to give me the lowdown on the competition. I'd had no idea she was related to the ever-so-well-adjusted and attractive Miss Ski Smithers. I mean, Miss Ski Smithers seemed so . . . normal. If I looked closely, I thought I could see the resemblance. Both girls were pretty, but where Miss Ski Smithers's hair was wavy, Emma's was electric. Where Miss Ski Smithers was lean and fit, Emma was gaunt and looked as though she raged off all her excess weight. And where Miss Ski Smithers's look was casually stylish in a timeless Audrey Hepburn-Gwyneth Paltrow sort of way, Emma had more of a former-child-star-of-bad-sitcom-right-before-checking-into-rehab look.

I thought Emma might be interested in hearing how the competition is actually about citizenship, and how her sister hadn't actually won it yet, but after consulting with Jesus decided not to. The pageant seemed to be a bit of a sore spot for her.

To change the subject I pointed at a line of red stickers leading from the curly-haired stick figure to one with a tiny beard, and Emma dropped her voice to a sinful whisper—"Red is for lust. Who do you think that is?"

Just then Bob opened his door, hand on goatee in his usual thoughtful, worried pose.

"Alice . . ."

I got up to go in but was stopped by a Puma runner grinding itself onto my foot. Emma stabbed a finger onto a sheet of green envy stickers and growled, "Don't make me add you to this chart."

Apparently her relationship with things biblical isn't as close as her hairstyle would indicate.

Later

Bob has not lost his power to disappoint me. He finally got hold of my 'zine and has decided that he was "extremely hurt" by what I wrote about him. I'm sure I didn't write anything *that* bad about him. I may have questioned his competency, suggested he dyes his hair, and detailed some of his less-successful therapeutic efforts. But that's about it. No matter. He said that we are going to have to work on rebuilding trust, and that my article could stop him from passing his practicum if it were to fall into his supervisor's hands. Then he said that he thinks he might be on the verge of a burnout– he asked me what the symptoms were–and I headed home via the private exit. As though it's any more embarrassing to leave a counselor's office than it is to hang around the front, waiting for an appointment.

Bob is just going to have to get over it. I've got my own problems to deal with. After I left his office, I pulled my sleeve over my Jesus bracelet and cinched it tight with my watch. Maybe I can muffle His demands a bit.

Goose has stopped calling and I hardly ever hear from George. All the other Miss Smithers candidates hate me due to my honesty. No one could say I don't know about suffering. There are probably certified martyrs who haven't been through as much as me.

February 17
I called George last night. I should have known bet-ter. I mean George is my best and only friend, and I can respect that she is not a phony or pretentious person. But she's a bit too prone to telling the truth and being honest about her feelings.

I told her about my new relationship with Jesus. In the course of the conversation I may also have mentioned that He doesn't approve of young people having sex with people they hardly know. She didn't take it well.

"Alice, did you just call me up to criticize my personal choices?"

"No. I just thought you might be interested in the Christian perspective."

"What do you know about the Christian perspective? Have you ever even been to church?"

"Well, no. But see, I've got this bracelet."

"This is a very intense time for me, Alice. I don't give a shit about your bracelet."

"That's a little harsh."

"Just because you're fighting with Goose, don't take it out on me."

"What? Take what out?"

"I like having sex. And I think I love Barry."

"But morally," I tried, "what would Jesus—"

Click. She hung up on me. What was her problem?

I have a lot to learn about saving people.

Later

Blows continue to rain down. I am being robbed of material for my 'zine. Tomorrow night the other Misses are going out for a social dinner without me, and my parents are going to the Ashley MacIsaac concert in Prince George! Without me! Here I have practically given up my life for Jesus and I am getting nothing in return. I am shunned. I am poor. What more could He want?

I thought Jesus was supposed to make the sacrifices. Not only am I being socially and psychologically destroyed by my leaked 'zine, I am prevented from making anyone pay for their unfairness by this shackle of a bracelet.

There has to be some way to get rid of it that won't land me in hell.

Other young people get to explore religion. But not me. Jesus Himself is holding me hostage.

A VEGETARIAN'S GUIDE TO DARKENED MEAT-EATING RESTAURANTS

February 18

I've been thinking about how to get one over on the other candidates and my parents, but my thoughts are clouded with compassion. The bracelet is working. This is very disturbing to me. It's worse than being muddled by confusion or frozen by fear. If this keeps up, I'll understand everyone's reason for doing everything. And next thing you know, I'll be walking a mile in their shoes.

No thanks!

Like right now for instance. I see it clearly. The other girls don't want me around because they are afraid of not fitting in themselves. Plus there's an outside chance they're still mad about the articles. George is walking her own life path and doesn't need interference from me. I basically broke up with Goose, and my mom and dad need some time away by themselves with their friends. How can I fault any of them? Only a monster could. But see, without this bracelet *I* could easily fault all of them.

All I can think to do is pout while my parents get ready to go. They're not even going to notice that. I really wanted to see Ashley MacIsaac. He's probably the only performer in the world we'd all like to see: me because he's a punk rock, kilt-wearing degenerate and them because he's a good musician. I am being forced into an emotional maturity beyond my years, and I won't stand for it. Jesus is going into the jewelry box and hell be damned! I'll put him back on when I turn thirty-five and I'm ready to see all sides of every issue. Or maybe I'll put him back on when I go to the Young Christian meeting to scope out Christian Mark. But right now I have some acting out to do.

Later

Finn picked up my parents around four o'clock, and I immediately went for my mother's Bad Thoughts Jar (she puts in a coin every time she has a mean thought). The thing weighs about one hundred pounds and she's only been adding to it for a couple of months. I think she planned to give the money to the deserving poor. Well, at least $50 is going to the deserving hungry—me and MacGregor.

I've decided that the best revenge is living large. Who cares about the other Misses and their dinner? I am a writer and a sophisticated woman of the world. So I'm taking me and MacGregor to Fat Freddy's House of Ribs. Let's see the other girls top that. I know this will be a meaningful growing experience because:

1) We never eat out in this family because my mom is into Small Is Beautiful and Simple Living and

Whole Foods and Mindful Cooking. No restaurant around here quite fits the bill–not multinational McDonald's, or Smitty's Pancake House, anyway. And my father's looks, his main contribution to the family fortunes, don't bring in much business, so we can't afford to go out for non-fast food.

2) My parents (or mother anyway, and she's the cook) are rabidly vegetarian. Unpleasantly vegetarian, actually. She's the kind of vegetarian who says things about other people's food, like "How's the dead cow?" or "Ever see the inside of a slaughterhouse?" At least that's what she says to me on the rare occasions I suggest we eat meat.

Interfering with my gastric pleasure like that is more or less abusive and has contributed a lot to my artistic qualities and inability to get invited out, I'm sure.

I've never actually been to Fat Freddy's, but I've gone by it lots of times. It's one of those no-windows meat restaurants. My theory is that when people are really getting in touch with their carnivorous selves, they prefer a cavelike atmosphere. I wonder if Freddy's has an open flame pit. Maybe once I'm a successful 'zine publisher, I'll open P. J.'s House of Meat, where people will squat on their haunches around a fire in a windowless room and eat red meat with their hands. I bet that would be quite successful. Those other girls are probably going out for salads and low-fat wraps. Hell, they're probably getting takeout Weight Watchers entrees or something. But not me. I'm going all the way.

I've told MacGregor we are dressing for dinner, so he's off finding clean cords. What I haven't told him is that we are *driving* to dinner. In for a penny, like we artists always say. Car theft, driving without a license, red meat: Here we come. Jesus must be having an attack in the jewelry box!

February 20

I am very ill. Meat-based rebellion is not what I thought it would be.

I guess when you grow up without eating red meat, it becomes hard for you to digest. At least that's what they told me at the emergency room.

The evening started well. I wore a simple black dress, which is what one wears for a night on the town. It was one of the many items I got on my thrifting trip to Prince George. It was originally yellow, so I dyed it black to better fit my new artistic personality. Unfortunately, it had a lot of Lurex or spandex or something in it, and the dye didn't entirely take. So it's a bit grayer than I would have liked. To hide the color, I put my extra-large Ramones T-shirt over the top. The T-shirt's quite long, so you can't see anything except the hem of the dress. Which is just as well since the dress looks pretty bad. My down-filled jacket put even more of a damper on the simple elegance of my little black dress, and by the time I had my silver moon boots on, it was hard to tell I was in evening clothes at all.

The car ride was relatively uneventful. MacGregor asked me a few times if I was sure I wanted to drive since the restaurant was only six blocks away. I reassured him, and once he'd reminded me how to start the car, we crept out of the driveway and turned down the first alley I could find. No need to attract attention. We drove from alleyway to alleyway and only brushed up against a few garbage bins. They made a lot of noise, but MacGregor, whom I'd told to belt up securely in the backseat, said no one came after us. It's a good thing, too. At the speed we were going, they could have caught us on foot. I've driven before, but apparently it's nothing like riding a bike. I couldn't remember the first thing besides gas versus brake.

It took a while to get across the highway, but MacGregor finally convinced me no one was coming. There were six or seven cars backed up behind us and they were honking and everything. One guy screamed out his window: "Any particular shade of green you're waiting for?" That as much as Mac yelling, "Go! Go!" spurred me across. Those kinds of high-pressure tactics are how accidents happen. If I ever get my license, I'm going to get an anti-road rage bumper sticker. I also have my eye on one that says "Hippies Suck." I thought it would be funny and ironic to put that on my mom's car.

We left the car next to the Dumpster behind Freddy's so none of my parents' friends would see it and went in.

Fat Freddy's House of Ribs was as dark inside as I'd hoped. We sat in the waiting area, peering through the inky blackness to try and get a glimpse of some of the meat. No luck. I could just barely make out the hostess stand in front of us, and knew only from my very limited restaurant experience that the indecipherable sign probably meant we should wait.

At last a brilliant white shirt came swimming into view. The hostess was right on top of us and I still couldn't see her face.

"Parents parking the car?"

"No. Um. It's just us."

Her teeth made an appearance above her shirt.

"So for two then?"

I nodded.

"Right this way."

We followed her shirt along an endless dark wood-paneled wall and turned the corner into the dining room. It looked how I imagine a church would, with all the silence and little candles flickering on each table. The salad bar gleamed off on the side of the room.

A few older couples sat bent over their food, utensils clinking softly.

The hostess left us at a table in the middle of the room, possibly so she could keep an eye on us. Good luck in this gloom!

When we were seated, I could barely see the outline of the top of MacGregor's head over the candle.

"So, what do you think?"

"Oh. It's nice" came his small voice from across the table.

The shape of a youthful person appeared at our table holding a water jug.

"Water for you here?"

Gender impossible to determine from voice. Visual cues unavailable.

"Yes, please."

Water went splashing more or less into our glasses, except for the ice cube that missed the mark, hit the table, and skittered into my lap.

I gave a little yell and jumped back.

"Oops. Sorry," whispered the water person.

A white rag appeared and made a jab at the table and then me, and I nearly tipped over backward in my chair trying to get out of the way.

"That's okay. Never mind."

The water youth disappeared and the waiter appeared. He was very charming and sounded as though he might be quite good-looking.

"Well hello! How are we this evening?"

This time I didn't lurch my chair back when his hand grabbed the napkin and settled it onto my lap. He really had a nice voice.

"And something to drink this evening?"

The evening's rebellion didn't include a drunk driving charge, so I decided against ordering a cran-tini, which is what one generally drinks when wearing a little black dress in a darkened meat restaurant.

In the murk he might have even brought me one.

"Shirley Temple for me." I had a whispered consultation with MacGregor, and finally managed to convince him that I'd brought enough money so we could have more than water and bread sticks. "Rob Roy for him."

Now we were getting somewhere.

"Very good, madam," the waiter pronounced.

Since it wasn't in Braille, reading the menu was out of the question, so I just guessed when he came back to take our order.

"And what can I get for you this evening?"

"We'll have steaks."

"Steaks? Any particular kind of steaks?"

"Um, you know. Big ones with mushrooms."

"May I recommend the nine-ounce with mushroom peppercorn sauce?"

"Yeah. That sounds good."

MacGregor said something indecipherable from across the table.

"What?"

"Can I just have the salad bar?"

"But Mac, we're going out for meat."

"I don't think I like steak."

The waiter assessed the situation.

"Perhaps some potato skins to go with his salad bar for the gentleman?"

The outline of MacGregor's head nodded.

"How would you like your steak done?" he asked me.

"Um—with peppercorns and mushrooms, I guess."

"I see. Medium well, then. And an appetizer for the lady? Perhaps a lobster tail with her steak or scallops wrapped in bacon for a starter?"

Lobster sounded fattening, so I went with the scallops.

We settled back to wait.

Strangely, all sorts of people started to come by our table. The hostess dropped by twice to see how we were, and the water youth must've checked our glasses three or four times. At one point a very large man who may have been Fat Freddy himself came by to say hello. The other customers made a point of walking past us, one at a time, even though the bathroom was on the other side of the restaurant. And this was before the food had arrived! This was some kind of full-service place!

Our waiter realized that MacGregor felt shy

going to the salad bar, so he made me take him. By this time we were on a first-name basis.

"Alice—may I call you Alice?—perhaps you'd like to take the young gentleman to the salad bar."

For some reason I didn't want to get up. I felt like everyone in the restaurant was looking at us. But I was the adult here. It was up to me to make the first move.

"Come on, Mac. Let's go look at the salad bar."

My metallic moon boots reflected every bit of light in the room as we walked over to the salad bar-mother ship. I wished I'd brought other shoes.

The salad bar felt like a stage.

"Aren't you going to get anything?" he asked.

"No. I'm okay. I'll just, ah, help you out here. So I guess you should, I don't know, get a dish or something."

Performance anxiety set in and I started to sweat. Where the hell were the plates? I couldn't see any dishes at all. I grabbed at the first bowl I saw, even though it was filled with spoons. Mac whispered, "I think that one's used." He finally found a plate in a stack at the end of the bar.

I continued trying to give him instructions. "So I

guess you just take stuff, you know, one of everything. I think you're supposed to get as much as you can on your plate. I don't know. Are you allowed to come back?"

I was really sweating now. I imagined people from other tables and various staffers standing just outside the light of the salad bar, seeing how incompetent I was in a salad-bar setting, how virginal and unsophisticated, how un-Miss Smithers.

I lunged and scooped a large spoonful of olives onto his plate.

MacGregor tried to hide his plate from my view while he put most of the olives back, and I took the opportunity to sneak back to the table, heart pounding, cheeks burning.

My appetizer arrived—scallops wrapped in bacon and baked in butter. They were quite good, and we got no fewer than eight visits asking us how our starters were.

I felt pretty full after the scallops, even though we were just beginning. I wasn't worried. I figured gluttony's sort of the point at a meat restaurant.

Three people came to clear our dishes—and a fourth put more candles on our table. We were now almost as well lit as the salad bar. A terrible thought occurred to me: Had someone recognized us as the offspring of the most annoying vegetarian in town?

My steak and Mac's skins arrived in a procession involving about six people. I've seen birthday cakes arrive with less fanfare. I'm sure I saw the cook and the dishwasher peering from the kitchen at us.

The waiter put our plates down. "There!" he exclaimed, and with the small forest of candles now on our table I could see that he was as good-looking as his voice suggested. How embarrassing.

Then all of them just stood there, waiting for us to begin.

The truth is, I'd never actually eaten a steak before. It's not that I haven't wanted to, I just haven't really had the opportunity to do anything harder than tuna.

I couldn't let these people down. Never mind that the thing in front of me used to be a cow's butt. This is Smithers. This is Fat Freddy's! Steaks are what we eat here. A true Miss Smithers would eat red meat!

I steeled myself, took a deep breath, and grabbed a knife. The waiter stepped in.

"If I may?"

He gently took the butter knife from my hand and replaced it with a heavy serrated knife.

The crowd sighed, relieved.

And I carved off a slice of that steak and ate it.

MacGregor stared at me with big eyes and gestured at one of his skins.

"You can have one of these if you want."

I shook my head, being careful not to choke on the piece of cow bum.

"No," I whispered. "This is fine."

Eventually, after I nodded and smiled at them, Fat Freddy's staff went back to serving the other customers and only checking on us every seven minutes or so.

Once I got past the thought of it, the meat wasn't bad. Neither were the baked potato, vegetables, coffee, and cheesecake.

I was having trouble breathing when it came time to pay the bill, so I gave the money to MacGregor and let him take care of it. We had just enough money for tax and a tip, and although everyone seemed disappointed when we left, it was good to get out of there.

The attention was nice and all but not really justified. I mean, maybe it would have been a big deal if a ten-year-old and a seven-year-old went out for meat. But by age sixteen a person is ready for an elegant dining experience.

The trip to the hospital afterward was nothing really. I was in a lot of pain but MacGregor, who seems to remember everything he's ever learned, including how to operate our car, drove very carefully. If fact, he drove so slowly that we probably could have walked there faster. The agony started to ease almost as soon as I met the nurse on shift and realized I'd be better off dying at home than in her unsympathetic care.

"What the hell didja eat?" was her idea of an excellent bedside manner. It was enough to make me glad when she handed me a package of Tums and sent me home with the comforting words, "Don't be such a pig next time!"

Our health-care system really is going down the tubes. When I'm feeling better, I'm definitely going to write a letter about it. Maybe even an exposé.

MacGregor was relieved that we got home before Mom and Dad. I wasn't worried. By definition an Ashley MacIsaac night is a late night.

February 21

The meat experience has reinvigorated my commitment to groundbreaking journalism. I'm going to keep writing, never mind the negative consequences. Dinner the other night produced, besides the stomachache, what surely must be the most insightful article of my 'zine career so far. I think it is evocative of a really interesting mind at work.

Meat Good at Fat Freddy's

Those of you thinking of good places to dine out on meat may want to consider Fat Freddy's on Main Street. It is quite dark, but the salad bar is well lit. The staff are very friendly and will help you if you need it. One waiter in particular is excellent.

Go prepared to eat meat, which isn't too bad once you get used to it. More young people should eat out, because going to restaurants teaches valuable lessons about life. Such as it doesn't matter

much what you wear if it's too
dark for anyone to see your outfit. So to all you girls who go to
bush parties every weekend, if
you aren't wearing your very
best, just stay out of the fire-
light and no one will notice. And
remember: If you just act like you
know what you're doing, you'll
probably be all right.

—P. J. Hervey

I already have plans, based on the hard-hitting success of that article, for a follow-up entitled "Meat:
What Is It Good For?"

So it looks like I'm back in the 'zine writing business. A little negative feedback can't stop a serious
journalist. I mean, look at that time a Hell's Angel
punched Hunter S. Thompson. Did he quit writing?
And look at all Ted Conover's been through for his
art! He's been chased by the cops and picked oranges
till he was very tired. He's even been to Aspen,
where he had to spend time with very wealthy
skiers. Well, I'm at least as tough as those guys. I'm

not going to be deterred by Miss Main Street's psychotic collection of head-banger cousins, or by the disapproval of anyone else. No one can stop a committed 'zinester like me.

MacGregor read the latest article and said it really captured the experience and that my description almost made him wish he'd tried some meat. Then he suggested that we pool our money to replace what I took from the Bad Thoughts Jar. He's right that it's probably a good idea to try to avoid what would surely be an unpleasant scene with Mom if she discovered the cash missing. For whatever reason, stealing is one of those things that she's quite uptight about.

Now I have to go and choose an outfit for school tomorrow. It's a special occasion—the Young Christian Association meeting—and I want to look my best. I'm thinking maybe I'll wear that old candy striper's smock I found at the Hospital Association yard sale. It looks like a sin-free garment.

THE ARTIST WHO FORMERLY
WALKED ALONE

February 22

This was the kind of day that could change the course of a person's life. I am being pulled in two directions by different social groups. Me! The Artist Who Walks Alone.

I put my WWJD bracelet back on and went to the Young Christian Association meeting. The YCs are the kind of people you'd want to know if you were ever going to have to spend time in the hospital. They'd probably visit every day, and they'd be fun visitors, too. I was pleasantly surprised to find that they don't really look that different from anyone else. Maybe they have a few more braids between them, but that's it really.

The most interesting thing about the Young Christian meeting was that Miss Ski Smithers was there. I've decided that she's the girl to beat in the pageant. She's luminously beautiful and, like the rest of the YCs, extremely nice. It's hard to believe she's Emma's sister.

I think Miss Ski Smithers is dating Christian Mark, which was disappointing for me, but I can forgive her for that because, like a true Young Christian, she is very gentle and accepting. She asked me to call her Esther and thanked me for the high scores I gave her on the chart. It was a relief to talk to her after all the negative feedback I've received. At first I couldn't tell if Miss Ski Smithers and Mark were together, because all the YCs are big on hugging and holding hands. The two of them, like everybody else, sang songs of love, praised Jesus, and planned good deeds. But when their eyes met, it was all business.

In fact, based on the heat of their glances, it is probably a good thing that they are going to take The Pledge with all the rest of the Young Christians. They were excited about a traveling chastity group that will be coming through town and how all the virginity-oriented young people are going to sign an agreement promising not to have sex before marriage. After reading my 'zine, they decided I'd be a good bet for lifelong virginity too. That's why they invited me to their meeting and gave me the bracelet. My lack of interest in sex may be overstated, but I am interested in this pledge idea, partly for 'zine research purposes, and partly because I can't let Miss Ski Smithers, or Esther, as those of us in the inner circle like to call her, get any more advantages over me. If she's going to be virginal, *I'm* going to be virginal. It occurred to me that George may have done IT first, but that won't mean much if I don't do IT at all. Ha!

I got home from the meeting and, inspired by Esther and her hot religious boyfriend's example, I immediately wrote a 'zine article with the idea of eventually leaking it to the Miss Smithers judges. Now that I've learned the power of leaked documents, it seems a shame not to channel it for my own uses. All I need is a distributor. Maybe I could get MacGregor to hand it out on street corners.

Waiting Until Marriage:
A Pretty Good Idea

If you are at all concerned about doing it and how embarrassing that might be, I recommend waiting. It's more acceptable to wait now. Not like a few years ago, when if you hadn't done it by age thirteen people wondered what was wrong with you. In the United States now there are large groups of otherwise normal youth who are eighteen and older who haven't done it, just because they aren't married yet. They say taking the chastity pledge has given them back the carefree childhoods denied their forefathers. I say this is just another example of how the United States has a lot to teach Canadians.

I personally have done a lot of praying about it and talked to my friends at the Young Christian Association, and we've decided to wait until we're married. After all, if one isn't having sex or thinking about having sex all the time, one has more time to do good works such as visiting the elderly, baby-sitting orphans, and fostering abandoned dogs.

Some people choose not to have sex because they are afraid of what some other people's parents might think. That's not a valid reason. Make the decision because

you want to be a better person and
so that you can be a better ambassador for your town.

In other words, Don't Do It for
Smithers!

—P. J. Hervey

February 23

I was still feeling extremely virtuous from the YC meeting when temptation struck. The devil sure doesn't waste any time targeting virgin Christians.

On my way to class I walked past the smoke pit and ran into Karen.

"Hey," she said.

"Hey. I mean, hi." I was all flustered that she was speaking to me in public.

"You want to check out a party on Friday night?"

I nearly dropped dead from shock. Karen Field was asking me if I wanted to go to a party with her Friday night. Me! If there is a social ladder, Karen is the top rung and I'm in the manufacturer's defect bin. In a hospital-stay situation Karen might stop by to throw down a used *Cosmo*, but that'd be about it, I figure.

She asked me to go to a cool person's party. With her.

I finally remembered to reply.

"Oh. Oh yeah. Sure. I mean, okay."

"All right. Pick you up at around seven. You live on Collingwood, right? That little brown house?"

Karen Field knew where I lived! She knew where I lived before I even told her. What did it all mean?

I walked away in a daze, feeling like Molly Ringwald at the prom. I'd been noticed!

Of course, a Karen party would involve drinking, drugs, sex, and a lot of hair spray, not to mention older men. Opportunities like this don't come up every day.

A Karen party is not something Jesus would attend, although he might stop by the next morning to see if there were any souls left to salvage. It goes without saying that no Young Christians will be in attendance. It's doubtful that any of the real contenders for the pageant will be there either. But I have a responsibility to my art.

Life was simpler when all I had to worry about was whether to sit beside my parents or my brother for Saturday-night videos.

February 24

My mother, snoop extraordinaire, found my chastity pamphlets–"Not Until Marriage," "Pure Partners–Guaranteed," and "Almost Like New"–in my pocket when she was doing my laundry.

She didn't know whether to be hysterical over the fact that I might take The Pledge or hysterical with relief that I hadn't filled out the "Almost Like New" form. As if that wasn't bad enough, she found my leather pants in my closet.

She rushed into the kitchen, pamphlets crushed in one hand, pants in the other.

"My God, Alice! Is this really what you want?" she asked, thrusting the handful of paper at me.

"I believe those are private documents," I said.

"Whatever. For God's sake, these people are trying to brainwash you."

"What people?"

"These virginity people. They're antiwoman. Antigay."

"No. They're anti-premarital sex."

Now she was stuck.

"Honey, I just think you'll be able to make the right decision for yourself without joining some -religious cult."

"So you want me to have sex before I'm ready."

"No! God, no. You're impossible. I just think there's more to these groups than you know."

"But I suppose it would be fine if I went to one of your nudist, whirling dervish, secret-paper-burning women's circles?"

"We aren't whirling dervishes. We are celebrating the earth, not asking for unthinking conformity."

"So if some woman showed up and wanted to keep all her clothes on and talk about makeup and the plastic surgery she wants to get, would that be okay?"

"That's not what we're about. We are celebrating freedom."

"So are the virgins. Freedom from sex."

As though she'd just remembered them, she held up the pants. "And these? What in God's name are these? What is happening to you?"

"They're for the Miss Smithers. I got them with my Rod and Gun Club allowance."

"But leather, Alice? Leather?" She looked stricken. "Do you have any idea what—"

I cut her short. "They're my pants. I don't want to hear about it."

She shook her head, disgusted and resigned.

"Jesus. I really don't know what's the matter with you. Why are you so determined to reject me and all I stand for?"

"If you'd stop going through my stuff, we wouldn't have these problems, would we?" I asked, with what I think was pretty lethal logic.

"I went in your closet to get your laundry, young lady."

At that she stomped off in her wooden clogs. When is she going to learn that her overinquisitiveness only leads to conflict? Wait till I tell Bob I'm being pressured by my own mother to have sex out of wedlock! He'll probably call social services.

February 25
Bob's reaction was extremely disappointing. Before I could tell him about my mother's unthinking advocacy of premarital sex, he wanted to talk about how I thought he was doing as a counselor now. Did I think he'd improved? Was I writing anything about him at the moment? When I finally got to tell him about my mother's inappropriate negativity toward virginity, he acted as though he didn't care. In fact, it was almost like he was on her side. Not only did he not call social services, for a second there I thought

he was going to call his own therapist to talk some sense into me.

Why is everyone so antivirginity in this town? It goes hand in hand with the twisted attitudes to drugs and drinking. It's considered almost as bad here not to drink as it is to be a falling-down drunk. The only difference is that at least the falling-down drunk will get invited to parties.

Bob asked me if signing a chastity pledge wasn't "a little extreme," particularly in light of my "developing" personality.

"I understand your desire to join a group. I really do. But perhaps the chastity group might be a little, um, constricting?"

"No."

"I see. Yes. Well, um, it's just that such a contract might, you know, complicate your, ah, later decisions in the event that you, ah, say, change your mind. You see?"

"No."

Bob got up and began to pace.

"I support you in your developmental decision. Of course I do. It's just that, well, ah, how airtight are these contracts?"

Bob is clearly an unmarried sex haver dealing

with his own demons. At the end of the session, which left him racked with conflict, I gave him an "Almost Like New" pamphlet. He was poring over it when I left out the wrong door.

Outside, waiting for her appointment, was the deeply troubled Emma. She sat sprawled in her chair in what looked like a five-year-old's T-shirt and hip huggers cut so low, you could see the waistband on her underwear. In a supremely un-Miss Ski Smithers gesture, she stuck out her tongue at me while she ran her finger lasciviously over the line of red lust dots leading to the Bob stick figure on her chart.

I hope for Bob's sake that he gives some serious thought to signing The Pledge immediately. I don't think he can afford to wait until the traveling virgins arrive.

Anyway, none of it is my concern. I have bigger fish to fry. Tomorrow night I am going to a party with Karen. I'll put Jesus in the jewelry box and let the dark forces take over. This must be what they mean by a balanced life.

February 26
In preparation to dive into the world of the popular people, I spent hours getting ready. It is very

important to fit in in these situations. I messed up my hair three different ways and put on and took off my makeup at least twice. I also, I'm ashamed to admit, tried to find the least thrift-looking of all my secondhand-store clothes. Eventually I settled on painter pants from the eighties, because I've seen some of the cool girls at school wearing something similar, and my not-even-secondhand glitter-front pink-and-white three-quarter-sleeve T-shirt that reads "Bitch, Bitch, Bitch." I figured older guys with jobs would be able to relate to the sentiment.

My mother started to get concerned as soon as she saw the hair spray.

"Are you going out?"

"Maybe."

"May I ask with whom?"

"Friends."

She was dying to know what friends but was afraid to ask. Instead she asked if she could come in and, without waiting for an answer, plopped herself onto my bed and sat, hands in her lap, tapping her feet on the floor.

"That one's nice," she said, watching as I added another pin to my hair.

"Can I help you with something?" I asked.

"No. No. So you're going out—" she said again with a pregnant pause at the end.

I ignored her and gave my hair another scrunch.

"And where were you going again?"

"Out."

This conversation was such a cliché, I was almost enjoying it.

"With?" she tried.

"Friends."

"Okay, Alice. I don't care where you go. Just tell me if you're going partying with the religious right."

"Ugh. Mother. For your information, I'm going out with Karen Field. Who smokes and drinks and has probably never seen the inside of a church."

My mother relaxed visibly.

"Well, okay then. Call if you need a ride home." Her relief was obvious. "You look nice, honey," she said, and left my room.

I finished getting ready. And then I waited. And waited.

I made sure I was waiting by the front window at seven o'clock, because I figured that's when parties probably get going.

By eight my parents were beginning to look worried and kept sending MacGregor in with unrelated-to-being-stood-up questions.

"Go ask her if she wants to come to the museum with me tomorrow."

MacGregor padded into the living room.

"Mom was wondering if you wanted to go to the museum tomorrow."

"No." Pause. "Maybe."

"Okay."

He padded back into the kitchen.

"Maybe," I heard him say.

Ten minutes later he was back.

"Mom wants to know what you'd like for your next birthday."

"I don't know. I haven't thought about it."

Back he went to report.

"She'll get back to you."

If this had been a real situation, and I hadn't just been gathering material for my 'zine, it would have been humiliating. As it was, I fought to maintain my detachment and to remember that I was a candidate with other commitments, such as the upcoming Etiquette Workshop. Still, I should've gotten off that couch at seven ten and made other plans.

But I was stuck. What if I got up to go to the bathroom and Karen came right then and it was some unwritten rule that cool people didn't knock on doors, they just honk or something? If I was in the bathroom, I wouldn't hear her and she'd leave and then she'd never invite me out again.

I tried to figure out why I cared about going out with Karen anyway. What was the big deal with her and her smoking-pit friends in their high-heeled boots and fancy hair?

I have, or at least I used to have, one friendship not just based on Christian kindness, a recently ex-boyfriend, and a whole group of new friends who may be compelled by God to hang out with me but are better than no one. So why did I care whether Karen showed up?

Why was I so aware she was cool? Why have I no integrity?

By nine o'clock I'd had enough.

"Mac!" I shouted to my brother in the kitchen, where he was playing Monopoly with my parents.

He came in.

"Want to play?" he asked hopefully, and my parents craned their concerned faces around the doorway.

"No, Mac. I want you to do me a favor."

Still unwilling to leave my watch post, I instructed him to bring me my most innovative and individual clothes. Sitting on the couch, I struggled into the late-1970s royal-blue terrycloth T-shirt with red piping, the brown cord jumper with multiple jean patch pockets, and brown leather wedgie boots with fur at the top.

"Mac. Get me my hat."

"Which one?"

"The brown cord one with sheepskin interior, Mac–the one with ear flaps."

"Okay."

He seemed thrilled to have something to do and returned carrying my hat.

"Here you go."

Transformation complete. Now at least I would meet rejection on my own terms.

After MacGregor went back into the kitchen, I heard the whispers as my parents asked him what was going on.

"She's changing."

"She what?"

"She's changing."

"But what's going on?"

"It's okay. She's okay," he reassured them.

I stayed on the couch until midnight. At ten my parents and MacGregor moved the Monopoly game out to the living room so I could play.

And at midnight I went to bed. Not exactly a successful night but I think I'm stronger for it. It's almost enough to make me take up writing poetry for my 'zine.

February 27

I am not a loser! Well, I am still a loser, but Karen's not! She called this morning to apologize for not stopping by last night. She and her boyfriend were having a fight and they broke up. But she hoped we could go out, maybe next weekend.

I pretended I barely even noticed she didn't show up last night. I even used the word "cool," as in "That's cool." That was sort of embarrassing.

And because I have all the integrity of mushroom soup, my mood instantly improved, which was also embarrassing. I just pray I get to go to one of Karen's parties at least once before I sign my chastity pledge. Just in case.

In spite of the premature publication of my 'zine and resulting renewed social ostracism, things are happening for me! I've been stood up by the coolest girl in school, I have a Jesus bracelet, I ate dinner at a steak restaurant and lived to tell, I may be a virgin until I marry, I'm a Miss Smithers candidate, and I HAVE LEATHER PANTS! I even feel ready for the first official event of the pageant, the Etiquette Workshop. MacGregor is online looking up the subject for me right now.

WORKING FROM THE OUTSIDE IN

February 28
Mrs. Kravchuck was an interesting choice to run a workshop on being ladylike. Rumor has it she's loose. This was the first time I'd seen her up close, and I saw no immediate signs of moral weakness other than she's got some kind of accent and wears her shirts cut low. I'd imagine it's common for people to be intimidated by a well-shaped older woman with a good grasp of cutlery.

She sat us all down at two tables at the Swiss Tea House. We had to pull out chairs for one another and sit with our legs together, in spite of the fact everyone but Esther and Miss Deschooling wore jeans. Some of the girls showed up looking downright slovenly, I think as a sign of disrespect to Mrs. Kravchuck. I noticed that Miss Deschooling continues her relentless march to self-improvement. She's added lipstick to her beauty arsenal. Esther better watch out: The Deschooling team looks to be gaining.

Once we were sitting down, Mrs. Kravchuck asked us to use the cutlery and dishes stacked in the middle of the table to "create a place setting with panache." My cutlery know-how is lacking because my mother specializes in vegetarian stews, so we rarely go beyond spoons in our house. I couldn't remember the place-setting layouts Mac printed out for me, so I just grabbed a few items and put them on either side of my plate.

Mrs. Kravchuck was shocked at our ignorance. Only Miss Panelboard Plant and Esther got it right. Miss Panelboard in her skintight track suit and high heels was motivated because she was in a hurry to join her boyfriend, who was loitering outside with his friend, making faces in the window and pretending to fart.

Esther was promoted to folding napkins into crowns at the counter, and Mrs. Kravchuck went around showing the rest of us how to lay out cutlery properly and explaining the order of use. Her large bosom dragged over the tops of our heads as she moved around the table. I saw Miss Forest Products fighting back a giggle when the wrecking-ball bosom knocked her glasses down her nose as she turned to ask a question. Miss Fall Fair caught the giggles too, and had to excuse herself to run to the bathroom, hooting and crying with laughter as she disappeared down the hall.

Once we'd learned how to set a table for soup, a salad, and a seafood course, Mrs. Kravchuck wrapped up the afternoon with a rambling talk she called "The Heart of the Hostess."

"Ees about confert. Ospitalité. Zee sense of zee senses, yes?"

No wonder the women of Smithers are intimidated by Mrs. K. I know my mother is not remotely familiar with any of these concepts, especially not "zee sense of zee senses." I bet my dad would appreciate them, though. My mother's approach to hospitality has always been more "Let's get to the wine and everyone can help with the dishes."

Luckily, hardly anyone mentioned my 'zine, although Mrs. Martin, the pageant chaperone, wearing yet another of what is apparently a bottomless collection of sweater sets, did seem a bit brusque with me, but that could just be my paranoia kicking in. Miss Bulkley Valley Fall Fair made a point of showing me her French manicure and telling me she could arrange for one for me. Miss Chicken Creek Fire Department came up to me afterward and said that I wasn't the only one who hadn't been invited out for the social dinner.

"I didn't get asked either," she said. "But I don't care. Because none of us would be in this contest if we were really cool."

I couldn't argue with that.

She looked over her shoulder, then continued. "I also thought your newspaper was hilarious. Even what you said on your chart was fair. Oh yeah, and the name's Nancy. God forbid I should be known as Miss Chicken Creek. That'd be embarrassing. Almost as bad as thinking decorum was jewelry."

I nodded. Nancy, you just earned yourself a few points across the board. You're up in the five range now, girl friend!

I was so filled with friendly camaraderie-type feelings, I wrote a 'zine article.

Etiquette: It's Not Just
About How Many Forks You Have
(Or Where You Put Them)

Who cares about etiquette anymore
except people with a lot of money
who go to fancy restaurants?
Practically no one.

But even if you don't have
enough matched cutlery to put
eight pieces around every place
setting, etiquette can still have
a place in your life. I hate moral
lessons as much as the next person, but it's important to realize that etiquette can be
extended to how you treat people.
In a sense, it's almost like
politeness that includes your
treatment of napkins.

At a recent Miss Smithers
event, some of the candidates
were openly disrespectful of the
hostess. They displayed poor man-

ners. Some candidates, on the other hand, went out of their way to be nice to others, thereby showing good manners.

In conclusion, even if you live in a small town where no one knows a shellfish fork from a butter knife, and have a dad who drinks soy milk right from the carton, you can always demonstrate your superiority by making an effort to be polite to others. It's an inspiring and democratic notion and certainly something to think about.

—P. J. Hervey

Later

All this should give me a few things to talk about when I go out with Karen. I'm not going to make the same mistake as last time. There is no way I'm going to spend hours getting ready. I will not betray my used-clothing esthetic just to fit in. An hour max should be sufficient for hair. And maybe another hour to try on every piece of clothing I own in different combinations. None of these three-hour get-ready sessions for me. I've learned my lesson.

THE MAIN STREET CHRONICLES

March 6

It generally takes at least a month of intensive togetherness for a person to be disillusioned by another, more popular person's lifestyle. I, as a prodigy, managed to reach that stage by ten last night. About the time that Karen and I were huddled in a ditch, hiding from an angry girlfriend and some kid's hysterical father.

If this is what life is like in the fast lane, I'm not built for it.

Karen arrived at around seven. I was surprised when she came to the door to get me, due to how polite that was, and also how difficult, since the truck she got out of was jacked up so high, I could see the outline of Hudson Bay Mountain between the oversize tires and the body.

"Hi, is Alice here?" she asked MacGregor, even

though I was standing right beside him in the doorway.

"Yesss . . ." he replied, with hesitation.

I didn't want him to get a whiff of Karen's boozy breath, which luckily was somewhat disguised by her hair spray, so I pushed myself in between them.

"Hi!" Too enthusiastic. "Hi," I repeated.

"Hello. Hey." Karen seemed to be having trouble focusing. "You got a bathroom I could use?"

I tried to whisk Karen by MacGregor. But she would not be whisked.

"Great house!"

Before I knew it, she'd plunked herself down on the floor in the doorway and begun to struggle out of her platform boots.

"Uh, that's okay. You don't have to take them off."

MacGregor stood in the living room looking worried and clasping his hands, obviously not sure what to do. My parents were out, and I think he felt responsible. The poor kid really has too much responsibility for his age. He should be doing science experiments, not worrying about his sister's dysfunctional social life.

Finally, Karen got her boots off and made it into the bathroom, where she had a bit of a fall, judging from the loud crash followed by silence.

I knocked on the door, praying she wasn't dead.

Karen swung the bathroom door open.

"Ready?" she said.

She was freshly lipsticked and smelled of mouthwash.

"Uh, okay. Are you, you know, okay?"

"Sure. Let's go."

Karen had pulled it together. Amazing. She barely staggered as we headed out the door. MacGregor's shoulders relaxed a bit, and he gave a little wave from the window as we crunched through the driveway gravel.

Behind the wheel of the truck sat the kind of guy I'd caught glimpses of but never seen up close or outside a vehicle with a roll bar and tiny lights twinkling up and down the running boards. He looked to be in his early twenties—old, in other words. He wore his baseball cap backward and had whiskers on his face, along with forearms that showed veins.

Karen clambered in and I followed. She rested her feet on the cases of beer sitting on the floor, then reached down between her legs, grabbed herself a bottle, and offered one to me. I noted with relief that the driver was not drinking. He looked like a consummate professional behind the wheel, like driving was all he really did, at least when he wasn't watching auto racing on TV.

"That's okay," I said to Karen.

She shrugged and twisted off the cap.

"Lonnie, this is Alice."

"How you doin'?" he mumbled without looking at me.

Was it uncool to ask where we were going?

The truck made my mother's ancient station wagon, which is almost suspension free, seem like a smooth ride. Every bump in the road our heads touched the ceiling of the cab. We rolled onto Main Street like three Mexican jumping beans in a Mason jar.

Oh my God. We were doing a Mainer! I was in a vehicle as it did a Mainer. Half shy, half thrilled to death, I almost couldn't believe I was involved in one of the most important rituals in Smithers Youth Culture. The Mainer is where it all begins—every party, every fight, and half of all relationships begin by driving up and down Main Street very, very slowly.

Tonight was no different. I think the experience may have been diminished a bit for me by the fact that all we could see from Lonnie's truck were the roofs of the other vehicles. It didn't bother Karen, though. She could still recognize everyone even from that height.

"Wait! That's Cheryl," she called. Lonnie slowed the truck to a stop, turned down the Def Leppard on the stereo, and opened his window. Karen leaned over him, and she and the occupants of the vehicle below pointed at each other and laughed hysterically.

Point. Point.

Hah, hah, hah.

Very mysterious.

Then she sat back and Lonnie took over negotiations.

"So whatcha up to?" he mumbled down to the driver of the other car.

"Pit. Checking out Bender's place first."

"Cool."

And that was it. Before he pulled away from the other vehicle, Karen would lean over and have another point-and-laugh session. Screams of laughter on both sides as we drove away.

After the third exchange Karen leaned back beside me and rubbed her head. She looked tired and depressed as well as drunk.

Maybe this was part of it–the Mainer burnout part of the ritual.

"Are you okay?" I asked.

For the first time since they'd picked me up, she asked me a question.

"What do you do at night?"

"I dunno. You know."

"No, seriously. You probably read or something, don't you? Hang out with your family. Call a friend on the phone."

"I guess."

"That's nice," she said, looking blearily thoughtful as she tried to peel the label off her beer, an impossible task in the swaying truck.

"Better than this," she continued, as we lurched from stop sign to stop sign and began to make our way precariously around the traffic circle by the government building at the end of Main Street.

Our Mainer was half over. I missed it already.

We started back the other way.

Suddenly a blue Honda, packed with people, pulled in front of us, blocking our way. The passenger door of the car flew open and a girl shot out, jean jacket and wild perm a blur, face a gnashing mask of eye shadow, teeth, and high-gloss lipstick.

"You bitch, Karen!" shrieked the Honda Banshee as she raced over to the passenger side of the truck, leaped in the air, let out a strangled yell, and kicked at the door, trying, I suppose, for a flying spin kick.

This was incredible! I thought that hanging with the most popular girl in school would get me away from this kind of sordid scene. Turns out attackers of popular people are just more athletic and marginally better dressed.

Drop Kick Girl had apparently miscalculated her abilities, and her runner was still a good half foot short of the door when gravity felled her like a sack of potatoes.

"Jesus," said Karen. "Not this again."

Before I could ask any questions, the raging girl's head popped up into our window.

"Bitch!" she had time to scream before falling off the running board again.

These monster trucks did have their uses.

Karen rolled down the window and leaned over

me to look down at the girl, who was outside winding up for another flying kick.

"Hey, Tammi. Little judo goes a long way, eh."

"Bitch!" Tammi spat again before launching herself at the door handle.

"Let's go," Karen commanded, and Lonnie eased the truck forward with the girl clinging to the door, huffing and puffing and trying to reach through the window and past me to grab Karen.

Karen leaned over me and rolled up the window, pushing the girl's grasping fingers one by one back through the gap.

A small cry as the girl fell off the truck. Oops, not quite. Her head popped up again as she struggled to maintain her grip on the side mirror.

The truck edged forward, and Karen opened the door just enough to dislodge the girl.

Thump.

"There she goes," said Karen.

This was Lonnie's signal to drive over the median, onto the wrong side of Main Street, and around the blue Honda, its tentacles of arms gesturing wildly at us through the open windows.

As we made our escape down a side street, a

hundred questions ran through my head. Lonnie eventually pulled over by the side of the road and disappeared out the driver's door, mumbling something about having to "drain the dragon."

"Sorry about that," said Karen.

"Who was that?"

"That's Tammi."

I stared.

Karen absently fixed her curls around her finger. "She's Lonnie's girlfriend. She thinks I stole him from her."

I looked at her.

"I didn't, though. . . . Lonnie and I are just friends. He's been driving me around since Kirk and I split."

"Shouldn't he tell her that? I mean, if she's his girlfriend."

Karen shrugged like it wasn't her problem and pulled out her lipstick.

Lonnie had acted as though he'd never seen the frantic flying kicker before.

Well, this evening with the cool people wasn't quite the glamorous good-times social whirl I'd imagined, but at least it wasn't boring. Baffling maybe, but not boring.

I wondered what the other candidates were doing tonight.

The next stop was a small house being taken apart by a bunch of kids.

The road leading to the house was lined with cars, people streaming out of them.

I started to get nervous. I'd been safe hidden up in the cab of the truck. But a public appearance like this was never a good idea for me. People might not realize that as a 'zine writer and Miss candidate, I should no longer be an automatic target for every kid with anger-management problems and an intolerance for alternative fashions. Karen was so wasted, she could barely remember who I was, much less protect me from the rougher elements. Maybe she and Lonnie wouldn't notice if I didn't get out of the truck.

"Let's go." Karen clambered over me and slid out of the truck and waited below me with the door open.

"I'll just wait here."

"Come on," she said.

"It's okay. Really."

"Hurry up." Karen wasn't registering my fear and resistance at all. It was useless. I was going to have to go with them.

Lonnie stopped to talk to some other baseball-capped men standing beside their big trucks, and Karen and I walked on our own up the drive to the pulsing house, Karen screaming greetings at everyone she met along the way. I breathed a prayer of thanks that so far no one had noticed me behind her in the dark.

Entry to the house was complicated by the fact that a group of boys had ripped the front porch away from the door. One boy was prying off wood siding with a crowbar. In front of the impromptu demolition team paced another boy. He clutched a phone receiver, from which the cord dangled uselessly.

When we got closer, I could see that he was trying not to cry. I could also see that he was too afraid to say anything to the other boys.

They grunted as they tore away at the house, only pausing to let partygoers swing themselves up to the orphaned front door. Someone lifted up Karen, and she held a hand back to me.

"Come on."

But I was frozen by the sight of the almost-crying

172

boy. I knew him. He was in my English class. He was quiet—not popular, not unpopular. And they were taking his house apart.

Karen disappeared, swept inside by the tide of arrivals. I stood in the dark trying to figure out what to do.

"Grant?" I ventured a guess at his name from a barely remembered roll call.

He looked around at me. The house behind us throbbed.

He rubbed his arm across his eyes and looked at me again. He had no idea who I was.

What to say?

When he spoke, his voice sounded hoarse.

"I am so dead."

"You want me to go get a neighbor or something?" I asked.

He looked over at the house's assailants, who were feeding the pieces to the party gods.

"I don't want them to set it on fire." He held out the phone receiver in a defeated gesture.

"If you want to go, I can stay here. And watch them, I mean," I said, wondering what I could do to stop them if they did decide to take a torch to it.

While we watched, the house spat out people.

They jumped from the door, some sitting stunned on the ground or giggling and rolling around together, others landing on their feet and weaving back toward the car-lined road.

The boy made up his mind. "Okay," he shouted, and ran down the driveway to get help, leaving me alone.

Where the hell was Karen? Where was I? No wonder I stayed home all the time. This was a nightmare. I was about to head into the woodshed to wait the party out when the nightmare got much, much worse.

A battalion of girls trudged up the driveway. They spoke in low rumbles. Even their laughter sounded as if it had bad grammar.

They saw me immediately. Damn these silver moon boots.

Suddenly all the people who hadn't noticed me before were on high alert. The tide of people leaving the house pooled and eddied around us as I was surrounded. In the crowd I saw Miss Panelboard Plant and Miss Forest Products with their boyfriends. When I looked over at them, they looked away, embarrassed.

"Hey! Is that what I think it is?"

"Well, well, well."

It was Head Bangs One through Ten, and with them was Linda, the girl whose sole aim in life was to make it unsafe for me to leave my house. She drove me out of school in first grade, and viciously attacked me last fall. Now she was probably going to kill me at my very first Smithers house party.

When I caught sight of her, my knees went stiff and fear seared its way down my back.

"Look, it's Princess Puke, the Newspaper Queen."

"The slut. Let's see what the freak's got on tonight."

Linda smirked while one of the girls grabbed at me, trying to pull my coat open. I wasn't going down without a fight. When Linda beat me to bloody pulp outside the Civic Center last time, I barely made even the lamest attempts to defend myself. No way I was going to allow that to happen again.

Another girl joined the first in trying to pull off my coat. I held it closed, clutching the halves together, grunting with the effort. One side of my coat slipped out of my hand, and the girl who held it wrenched it from my shoulder, spinning me around and knocking me down so I landed on my hands and knees on the hard ground, stubbled with frozen grass.

Gasping and numb, I stood up again, coat hanging from the crook of one elbow, feeling as though my shoulder must be broken. Linda moved in front of me.

She stood with a beer in one hand, cigarette in the other. Taking a last drag from her smoke, she flicked the butt into the crowd.

"Ow!" screamed someone.

I tried to say something, but my crashing heartbeat, which seemed to have moved up into my vocal area, prevented it.

"I told your cousin I wouldn't kick your ass no more," slurred Linda, wiping the back of her mouth. Linda'd gone on a crime spree with my cousin Frank a few months ago while Frank was visiting our family. They'd stolen a neighbor's car and driven to Nelson, where they probably planned to start their own grow operation or maybe a meth lab. They were eventually arrested after skipping out on their bill at ABC Family Restaurant. Apparently somewhere along the way Frank convinced Linda to stop terrorizing me.

Linda moved in closer, pulling the crowd with her.

"But I didn't say I wouldn't have a drink with you."

She lifted the beer bottle over my head and poured. The liquid ran in a yellow foaming river down my face, burning my eyes. When it was empty, she let the bottle fall with a dull clunk onto my skull.

I tried to wipe my eyes. So far my defensive tactics hadn't been too impressive. One of the Miss Main Street boosters said, "Who's not on the chart now, Psycho Girl?"

Something in me snapped. God, the devil, who knows. I just couldn't let this happen to me again. Slowly I straightened my arm and let my coat fall to the ground.

"Screw you," I muttered.

The girls, who had been moving away, stopped.

"Holy shit," one of them said, incredulous. "Did it say something?"

I lifted my head, my face a sticky mask.

"That's right."

"Hey Linda. It's talking back."

Linda, who'd been leading the pack away, stopped.

"What?"

"She's calling you down, Lin. She's giving you lip," chorused the bloodthirsty voices.

Linda stalked back to where I stood.

"What did you say?" she demanded.

Fear made my knees knock together painfully. Come on, voice: work! Say something.

"Whatever."

That was my comeback, my big statement. Not exactly John Rambo telling her she'd drawn first blood, but it was the best I could do.

The slap was instant and felt like someone had touched my wet face with a hot iron.

"That's it, Linda! Bitch slap her!" howled the crowd.

No way I was going to the Miss Smithers events with a black eye. Linda moved to slap me again and I held up an arm.

A lone voice in the crowd called, "Good block!"

And I managed to block blows three and four too. But I wasn't so lucky with number five. It came in low and hit me in the stomach. I doubled over, lungs slamming closed in my chest. I dropped to my knees and tried to reverse the flow of air back into my screaming lungs.

"Pussy," said Linda before walking away. I heard one of her crew say, "You went easy on her this time, Lin."

"Ah, I'm too pissed to deal with it."

As I crouched on the ground, a pair of high heels walked into my visual field.

"You okay?" asked a voice that sounded suspiciously like Miss Forest Products.

I nodded, still unable to speak, surprised that she'd ask after my health. I figured she'd be more the type who'd kick me on her way by. I tried to look up to see who the shoes were attached to, but they were already gone.

Then a pair of large boots walked into view and a hand descended and put something in the pocket of my coat, which lay in a heap beside me.

The deep voice above me said, "Not bad defensive moves. You should stop by the club sometime." And then the boots too moved away before I could see their owner.

When I was finally able to move, I was alone, rooted in place with frozen sticks of beer hair hanging in front of my face. It was over. No serious injuries, just a raw cheek, a sore shoulder, a bruised midsection, and crunchy hair.

But where was Karen? The deserted house put up a brave front behind me, every window brightly lit and the stereo on full blast. I dragged the dislocated porch and stairs over to the front door and climbed up, avoiding the missing slats.

The front door was open and I stepped inside. Every surface was covered with bottles and cans, the floors and counters studded with crushed cigarette butts. In the living room a dead boy lay beneath an overturned couch. I peered more closely. No, not dead, just passed out.

Had Karen just left me here? Had she just walked past me in my hour of need and decided not to get involved? I couldn't believe she would do that.

A boy left a room at the end of the hallway and hurried past me. I waited a moment and then went into the room he'd just vacated. Karen lay inside, asleep on the bed, an arm thrown over her face.

"Karen?"

She lay motionless.

I switched on the light.

"Karen?"

She bolted upright.

"I've got my pride!" she yelled.

"I'm sorry?"

Medusa hair everywhere, obscuring her vision, she groped for her drink on the headboard shelf, took a deep gulp, and slurred, "Piss off. I'm not into it."

I got the feeling she wasn't talking to me.

"Karen, are you ready to go?"

She lifted her hair back from her face like she was parting curtains.

"Alice?"

Oh man. She was so out of it.

"Come on, Karen, let's go. We have to get out of here. Everybody else is gone."

"I have my pride," she repeated, now fumbling around on the bed for her shoes.

Even my parents' friends were more coherent than this on a Saturday night.

I got her coat on her and helped her outside. If this was the care Lonnie took of his nondates, then he deserved Drop Kick Tammi.

We'd just made it down the detached stairs when the driveway was stabbed by headlights and buffeted by the roar of engines. Grant's neighbors to the rescue. Me and my frozen beer head, I knew, weren't exactly the picture of innocence, and the drunken Karen was none too impressive either, so I dragged her, still mumbling about her extreme pride, behind the woodshed.

"Shhh!" I admonished her.

Slam! Then in quick succession: Slam, slam, slam.

"What the hell!" barked a voice. Deep, male. The owner of the house? He sure sounded angry enough.

"Stan, I came over as soon as Grant told me what was going on." Another male voice. Not as angry.

"Jesus Christ! Would you look at this goddamn house."

"Looks like they're gone."

"Goddamn kids. I find them, I'm gonna kill them."

I heard the door of the woodshed creak open, and the sound of something sliding off the wall and the unmistakable click of a gun. A gun! He was getting a gun!

I was sick with the irony of it, for the 'zine headline I'd never get to write: "Miss Rod & Gun Club Shot to Death After Party at Gun Nut's."

Footsteps moved up the stairs, then a loud cracking noise and a strangled cry as a weakened stair broke.

"Jesus H. Christ," came the voice again, and then it really started swearing.

This was our chance to get away.

"Come on!" I tried to wake Karen up.

"Crawl!" I hissed at her when she tried to stand. "Crawl!"

A thump behind us as the sleeping boy was ejected from the house.

Footsteps pounding down the stairs after him.

"Now, Stan. Don't hurt him. The cops'll look after him."

Oh my God! Grant's dad was killing stragglers.

On hands and knees we reached the ditch that ran alongside the road.

"Stay down! Keep moving." My hands felt frozen and my knees were on fire. I prayed no one would see our retreat. I would have hated word of this to get back to the other candidates, or God forbid the Miss Smithers judges.

There, still parked in its original spot, was Lonnie's truck. The hood was propped up, and Lonnie, that prince, stood on the front bumper with his back to us, looking into the engine. The chauffeur without a clue.

"Hey!" I hissed up at him. "Help me get her up."

Lonnie jumped off the bumper and let down the hood of the truck with a crash.

"Quiet!" I whisper-yelled. "They'll shoot us if they catch us." This last bit may have been high drama on my part, but better safe than sorry.

Lonnie pulled the legless Karen to her feet and

watched, stupefied, as I crawled over to the passenger door, climbed up to reach the handle, and finally managed to get it open. He pushed her up into the truck, and I dragged myself in after her. Thank God we'd parked so far down the road. We could turn the truck around without going by Grant's house. One look at Lonnie's idiotic truck, and Grant's dad would probably start sawing the barrel off his shotgun.

When we'd put about ten minutes between us and the house, Lonnie spoke up.

"Yeah, so you wanna check out the gravel pit?"

Yeah right. If that was a house party, I can't even imagine what a pit party would be like. As a candidate I really can't afford to attend any more unsanctioned events.

I made Lonnie take Karen home before he dropped me off. I didn't trust him to do it on his own, and I hated to think of her passed out in his truck outside some automotive shop all night.

He unloaded her and walk-dragged her to her door. I checked to make sure he didn't just leave her on her doorstep.

When he dropped me off, it was a shock to find my family still awake and playing Scrabble in the kitchen. I felt like I'd been out for days.

184

"Hi, honey!" my mother called from the kitchen.

"Come and help us stop MacGregor from making us look like fools," yelled my dad.

"In a minute." I hurried down the hall to the bathroom before they could get a look at me or smell my beer-soaked hair.

After a quick shower I got into my pajamas and went to watch MacGregor rout my parents.

I dodged awkward questions and comments— "So did you have a good time?" and "You're quite the social butterfly now"—feeling grateful that at least I didn't have any real wounds to explain.

"It was okay" was all I said, and I wondered how Karen was.

March 8

Karen apologized today. Sort of. I passed her and a couple of her friends in the smoking area as I was coming out of class.

"Hey, A. What's up?" she asked.

What is the etiquette here, Mrs. Kravchuck? Was I supposed to do an intervention of some kind? Ask her just what was going on? Pretend I hadn't noticed anything strange about her behavior on Saturday night? What would Jesus do?

"Thanks for looking out for me the other night."

"Yeah. Are you okay?"

"Sure."

Her friends played with their hair and spoke in two-part harmony.

"She get whaled on ya, Al?"

"Ha ha!"

"She's always like that."

"Every weekend."

"Her boyfriend–"

"Used to baby-sit."

"Lonnie's not up to it, eh, Kar? He's a little lacking in the brain power department–"

"–all he's got is horsepower, eh, Kar?" whinnied the Two Stooges.

Karen sighed.

"Spinny bitches. See you later, A."

"Yeah. Later, A.," repeated the others as they walked past me.

Yes, popularity certainly appears to have its drawbacks, not the least of which is excessive name abbreviation.

I called George tonight to talk, which I thought was a pretty big gesture on my part, since she's hardly been a very good friend to me lately. But she

was out. On a date. Unpopularity has its own drawbacks.

Oh well, at least I have my art.

The Main Thing About Mainers

Sure, it might start out all
right. You get in your grossly
overheight vehicle and drive up
and down Main Street. Smile and
wave at your friends, make plans
to meet up later. The ritual is
harmless. Traditional.

But here's the rub. While you
aredriving up and down Main
Street, you are not only using up
gasoline and doing your part to
heat up the earth, you are also
making yourself a target for
every spin-kicking psycho in town
with a grudge and a good grip.
Plus your plans will likely land
you at a house party where nothing good could possibly happen.

One minute you're on Main

Street, harmlessly polluting and socializing, the next you're participating in a heinous vandalism of someone's home, and you, a nice, interesting person, have been rendered stupid by alcohol. Can you see the connection?

If you are a young person whose life lacks excitement, consider joining a sport such as tennis or perhaps softball. It might keep you off Main Street and out of trouble. And if you really must cruise Main Street, consider riding your bicycle. You'll see more and, hopefully, be too tired to pedal all the way to the horrific-house-party conclusion where front porches are destroyed and illusions shattered.

Consider it a friendly warning.

—P. J. Hervey

SCOTLAND THE BRAVE

March 9

We watched *Braveheart* tonight, and it sent my mother into a fit of ethnic pride. Every five minutes or so she exclaimed, "Oh, this is far too violent. Alice and MacGregor really shouldn't be watching this." And in the next breath she'd be bragging about our Scots heritage.

"You know, we come from a proud old Highland clan. The MacLeod family motto is 'Hold fast.'"

I was actually interested, so I asked her about it.

My dad snapped, "Oh no. Not another one who's going to use an incredibly tenuous and largely fictional Scottish connection to shore up her sense of self."

"Just ignore him, honey—he's having some trouble with the Magic Marker. You know how he is with tools."

My father was annoyed because he was trying to watch the movie and hand-write a flyer for a new musician, and his multitasking abilities weren't up to the job. He has decided that he is understimulated due to residing mainly in the basement, and his remedy is to "get the old band back together." My mother's very excited at the prospect, because it means a chance for her to relive her sordid groupie past. She loves to tell about how when she met my dad, he was the lead singer for a band called the Hoar Hounds and he was so handsome all the girls were interested in him. God, Mother. Must we discuss these things? Needless to say, I foresee great and possibly crown-destroying embarrassment in my future as my father and his hair-impaired (too much in the wrong spots, too little in the right ones) band mates run around town rehearsing and, worse, auditioning for such glamour gigs as the Fall Hockey Dance.

My mother continued, "I'm glad you are interested in our Scots ancestry. We have a long and proud history . . ."

My dad, having just made yet another serious spelling error, growled in frustration.

"Diane, I thought your parents were English. You know, Lowlanders and all that."

"They are not. We're from the Clan McDonald."

"The Clan McDonald of Nelson, B.C., maybe."

"Are you suggesting we aren't as Scots as the MacLeods?" My mother looked ready to drop the gloves, pull his sweater over his head, and give him a pummeling.

"No, I'm just suggesting that once a family has been in a country for a couple of hundred years and interbred with every other nationality in the world, it seems a little ridiculous to hang on to some kind of mostly fictional ethnic identity."

"Not when you're a Scot," she said, obscurely but with great conviction.

Our family has been in Canada for about as far back as anyone can remember, but that doesn't mean that when the going gets tough, the tough can't go back to their distant roots. It occurred to me that being a sort-of Scot might be useful in some way, like in giving me a sense of identity that stretches beyond being the underprivileged child of small-town ex-hippie parents. Whatever my future may bring, I'm going to try and incorporate plaid and the bagpipes.

By the end of the movie I had a good appreciation for our warlike heritage. In the absence of a fierce Highland clan to join, I got another idea for protecting myself. I remembered the card left in my jacket pocket after the assault at the party.

It reads:

K. A. Martial Arts
Kung Fu
Karate
Muay Tai
Jujitsu
Kick ass and have fun with Shawn!
e-mail: asskickerdojo@bulkleyvalley.net
phone: 250-555-2223

I can't even summon up the energy to pretend that my interest is for research purposes. At this point learning self-defense is a matter of survival.

I've tried the path of religion and so far it hasn't helped. I'm still getting beat up. And to be quite honest, the Young Christians are nice, but they don't seem all that focused on me as an individual. I'm more of a cause or a project than a person. Oh sure, they're concerned about my soul and my virginity. But the mess that is my true self they barely seem to notice.

We Scots are a fierce and proud people. Well, this Scot in particular has had enough of being a punching bag for people who were probably *never* Scottish, not even two hundred years ago.

Later

Shawn answered on the first ring.

"Yeah?"

"Is this um, K. A. Martial Arts?"

"Yeah."

"Ah, so, do you, like, give lessons or something?"

"Across from the Friendship Center. Seven thirty Wednesdays."

And the phone went dead.

I guess asskicker Shawn isn't in the business of mollycoddling the clients, but I would have liked to know what to wear, at least.

BETTER TO BUILD A GIRL
(THAN MEND A WOMAN)

March 10

The K. A. (or Kick Ass) Martial Arts dojo is, as the name would suggest, not a place for the cowardly. It took forever to decide what to wear. After much agonizing I decided that sportswear was the thing. Probably a classic gray tracksuit would have been best, but all I had were my red-satin shorts with the

193

white trim and a green nylon sleeveless basketball jersey worn over a white tank top for modesty. The green jersey is supposed to look a bit Celtic to give me ancestral strength. Obviously I would have gone for a tartan jersey, but I couldn't find one.

The club was located, as Shawn said, right across from the Friendship Center, which is the local meeting place for the First Nations people in Smithers and those who wish they were First Nations people. Shawn himself answered my knock by flinging open the door and barking, "Come in and line up!" He made those warriors from *Dances with Wolves* look like weakling cowards. He had long, straight black hair worn in braids, and rippling chest muscles visible under his white pajama jacket, and he appeared to be approximately eight feet tall.

I scurried into the room trying to be inconspicuous, which was tough since everyone else was wearing white. The dojo consisted of one large room with no windows. Inside, three groups of students were lined up according to size and age. The really young kids stood at the front of the room, the older ones in the middle, and the teenagers and adults at the back. Miss Moricetown stood, looking fierce and not at all happy to see me, in the tall group. When I glanced her way, she stared right through me. In fact, the older lineup as a whole gave me such a stare when I went to join them that I retreated to the middle line, which looked to be made up of ten- to thirteen-year-olds.

Shawn stood in front of us, and suddenly everyone else sank to their knees and bowed. By the time I got down, everybody else was back up again and sprinting, barefooted, around the room, trying to catch Shawn.

I took off after them, fighting off worry about damaging my North Star runners, which are collector's items, after all.

"Drop! Give me five," called Shawn.

Everyone else had done three sit-ups before I had completed one.

"Run!"

A couple of people tripped over me where I lay on the floor, struggling to finish my sit-ups. I got up after four, to avoid being trampled. Shawn noticed.

"You! In the green! Give me one more! And take off those shoes."

Ugh.

The rest of the warm-up included painful inner thigh stretches and Shawn walking on the older students to test their abdominal strength.

When Shawn told us to get in our groups, I hesitated.

"You," he said, "come with me."

I tried not to stare at his perfect chest as he asked me questions.

"Have you done any martial arts before?"

"No. No, I don't think so, really. Well, you know, I've watched Bruce Lee movies. Ha ha."

Shawn was unmoved by my attempts at humor. He was a very serious person.

"That's jeet kun do. We don't teach that here."

"Oh. That's okay."

"Why are you interested in the martial arts?"

What a question! What could I say? So I could leave my house to attend school functions without an armed escort? Because my cholesterol is too high? Because I am Scottish?

"Uh, self-defense, I guess."

He gave me a hard look, and I dragged my eyes from his chest to his eyes. He was even better looking than Mr. Mother Teresa. I reminded myself that I prefer my men funny-looking.

"Self-defense is a good motivation. Discipline and hard work are even better. The martial arts are not to be used lightly. The better the warrior, the fewer the fights," said Shawn.

"Right," I said, as though I knew what he meant.

"You'll work with Jeff for the first few lessons. Then you will be ready to join the intermediate group, the Bees."

"The Bees?"

Shawn pointed at the middle group of kids.

"You are too tall for the Butterflies."

"The Butterflies?" Whatever happened to black belts and brown belts and all that?

"It's from that quote by Ali. Float like a butterfly, sting like a bee. The most advanced group are the Bears." He continued, "We don't use the belt system here. We're a mixed martial arts club. Nondenominational."

He was not smiling when he said it.

It's too bad I wasn't going to get to fight the little kids in the Butterflies. I might've had a chance against them.

Shawn looked me up and down, but not in a confidence-enhancing way. "And ask Jeff where to get a gi."

With that he was gone, and in his place stood a

muscular, crop-headed, flush-faced boy wearing a grin that threatened both ears. He looked about eighteen and must've already graduated, because I'd never seen him around school.

"Hi. I'm Jeff," said Mr. Enthusiasm. "Saw you getting your ass kicked last weekend. Glad you decided to come out."

Nothing like leaving me a few shreds of dignity to wrap myself in.

"So you put that card in my coat?" I asked.

"You bet!" he boomed. "Thought you could use a little training. Get those low blocks working for you."

I felt tired out just looking at Jeff, and we hadn't even started yet. The energy reserves seemed to drain out of my body and straight into Jeff until sparks shot out the top of his head and his skin took on an atomic glow, leaving me empty and just barely able to support the weight of my vaguely Celtic workout gear.

"Okay!" he shouted. "Let's try a kata."

"A cut-off?"

Jeff was so pumped, he didn't hear my question. He leaped, muscles bulging, into some kind of weird stance with his chin tucked into his chest, his legs apart, and his arms crooked in front of him.

"Like this," he said, without moving his chin from his chest.

If I had thought I could get away, I would have made a run for it then. What did I want with some cut-off? The only way that stupid maneuver would help me is if future attackers died of laughter before they got a chance to pulverize me.

Reluctantly, I arranged myself into a mirror image of Jeff.

"Hey, great!" he said. "Now do this." One of his arms went up and the other went down.

I copied him.

"Not bad at all."

He switched his arms back in a reverse of the last move and then shifted so his torso faced the side while he did the motion, and each time I followed his action.

"Shit," he said admiringly, "you're a natural."

Jeff told me the names of the arm movements— high block, low block, and side block—and then he demonstrated how they were meant to be used.

"So say, you know, Linda or one a them is comin' after you," he speculated, an unnerving excitement in his voice, "and she goes to give you a shot in the head like so." He pretended to punch me in slow motion.

I didn't even think about it, my arm just flew up and knocked the incoming punch away.

"Right on!" Jeff was thrilled.

I practiced blocking high, low, and medium shots until my forearms stung. At one point Shawn came by and nodded his approval. Jeff looked proud.

It seems as though I may be good at something, and I have to say it's about time. I have been inadequate in almost every area for long enough. It's my turn to have a talent, even if it's only blocking shots to the head. I can see a celebrated career as Miss Mixed Martial Arts just over the horizon! World Blocking Championships, here I come! Braveheart himself would be proud.

I would write a 'zine article about my new sport, but my arms are too worn out. My art may have to give way to my athletics, sort of like how religion is taking a backseat to self-defense for me these days.

ANTICLIMAX

March 15
Not wanting to give up on the Young Christians as a peer group entirely, I went to meet the celibacy bus today. It was quite an anticlimax.

The bus was parked right next to the railway station. I expected to find the area swarming with virginal youth, but when I arrived, there was no one in sight, not even the Young Christians. No happy virginity music was being piped outside to draw the people, no dancing celibates looking fulfilled anywhere in sight. Just an old yellow bus with the words *Purity & Chastity* faintly visible under the mud and dust caking its sides.

I walked around to the door, expecting to find a lineup of pledges. But it was just me, alone, outside an empty bus—a virginity groupie apparently without a group. I started to feel sort of pathetic—the only virgin in town going to make it official.

I clutched my signed virginity pledge card in my hand. I'd given my name and address and checked the "yes" box next to the line that read "I will be a virgin until I'm married!" and signed my name.

I walked all the way around the bus once more. Still nobody. This was enough to make me run out and have premarital sex from sheer disappointment.

A grizzled Canadian National Railway worker with slicked-back gray hair leaned against his crew cab, smoking and watching me circle the vehicle.

"Nobody home?" he asked.

I shrugged.

"Seen a groupa them heading out 'bout a half hour ago. Said something about goin' to St. Joe's for tea. Meeting some group of kids there for some church ceremony."

He ground out his cigarette with his work boot.

"I 'spect they'll be back soon enough."

Oh man. It figured. Left out again. The YCs forgot about me. I'd missed the celibacy bus. The story of my life.

"Thanks," I muttered to the CN guy, and tried to decide whether to sit and wait or give up and go home.

This was ridiculous. I thought I'd be supported in my choice to be virginal until marriage. In fact, I expected to be celebrated, made much of, held up as an example. And here I was, alone. Exposed.

"Yer the first person I seen come near the thing."

CN guy was enjoying our lopsided conversation.

"Course it's only been here a day or so," he mused. "What's it for, anyway?" he asked. "Looks like nice folks running it."

"Oh, you know. They're running sort of like this contest."

"Yeah?" Now he was interested. "Like a lottery or something?"

"Sort of."

"What's the prize?"

Good question.

Without thinking, I told him the prize was a house.

"No kiddin', eh? A house! Them tickets must be some pricey."

"Free, actually."

"No shit. 'Scuse my French, but that's rare these days. Last lottery I entered for a house, one of them dream homes on a flatbed down at the Fall Fair, the tickets cost me damn near two hundred dollars apiece. But these are free, eh?"

I nodded.

"So what's a guy gotta do to enter?"

"Name and address on a piece of paper."

He felt around in the chest pocket of his plaid shirt for a pen and then explored his work pants for a piece of paper.

"Don't mind if I do," he mumbled to himself.

I slipped my pledge into a gap under the door of the bus and walked away. Mr. CN was right behind me.

"Good luck!" he called as I walked away.

"Yeah, thanks," I replied.

"Hey—maybe there's two houses, eh? We'll keep her our little secret and we'll each get one—you'll get Chastity 'n' I'll get Purity!"

"You bet." I made a gesture like I was zipping my mouth and walked away wondering how binding his pledge would be, made as it was under false pretenses.

Later

I was right. I missed the chastity bus, or at least the chastity-pledge ceremony. Christian Mark called me tonight to ask where I'd been. I guess I misunderstood the instructions. Like the CN guy said, the virgins met at St. Joe's, where they had tea and handed in their forms and, I imagine, got a lot of positive reinforcement for their healthy decision. They didn't spend the afternoon with a railroader looking for free merchandise.

Mark asked if I at least handed in my pledge. He sounded relieved when I said I had.

"We want to keep you with us, Alice."

Ha! If they wanted to keep me with them, they'd have made sure I had proper directions to the ceremony.

"Oh sure. Absolutely. I'm with you," I said,

which was a lie. I think I'm done with the YCs, as with so many other things in my life, such as large, drunken house parties. Let me down once and you don't get another chance. Unless you're Karen and very cool.

March 16
The Bonding Over Beauty event is coming up soon, and then a few days after that is the fashion show. The Bonding event involves getting our hair done and sharing our favorite beauty tips. It should be interesting to see what some of the contestants come up with. I'm not holding my breath that anyone's going to give me the tip I need to catapult me into being voted one of *People*'s Most Beautiful People.

It's a toss-up whether I'm nervous or excited for the fashion show. I mean, for the past while I've been quite fashionable or at least paid a lot of attention to clothes. Maybe it will be my breakthrough event!

I doubt my speech for the Mother-Daughter Tea and Speeches will do much for my place in the standings. I've been practicing, and it's not going well. We are supposed to introduce ourselves and say why we want to be Miss Smithers and talk about what we can contribute to the community. Our talk is supposed to last about five minutes. I can't seem to stretch it past one minute; two if I repeat everything. But too short or not, the speech is somewhat doable and so is the Miss Smithers Charity Curling Bonspiel. It's the talent show that I'm really worried about. How did I get so old and not manage to pick up a single demonstrable talent along the lines of tap dancing or baton toss? It's quite tragic and speaks to my deprived homeschooled childhood. It would be cool if I could do a girls-with-guitars type thing. But if the success of my short-lived piano lessons is any indication, a performance involving a musical instrument is not a good idea. I'm sure something will come to me. This pageant business really does require a well-rounded individual with a lot of time on her hands. I'm going to acknowledge that, when I finally get around to updating the Miss Smithers Chart.

Bob and I had one of our rare catch-up sessions today. Those are the ones where we actually talk about me. He was very impressed with all my news. He said he feels like I am really making strides—giant steps he called them. He was distracted from my virginity pledge by the minor assault by Linda at the house party. He was all set to put the empathy into overdrive until I told him it wasn't that big a deal. I've been beaten up properly. I know the difference.

Bob didn't know what to make of the big meat-eating adventure or what to say when I told him I'm replacing religion with a course in self-defense. I froze him out when he asked about my writing and why George and I aren't speaking much anymore. When he asked how Goose is, I said he was fine. I didn't mention that I blew it with the only man I've ever loved. Bob's counseling skills aren't equal to dealing with that kind of tragedy.

So all that was left was to focus on the pageant. He wanted to know who I thought would win and what I was going to do for my talent and what Miss Ski Smithers is really like (a clear violation of privacy and possible conflict of interest).

Bob lacks focus, but you could never fault him for lack of enthusiasm. He has rebounded nicely from the comments I made about him in my article. He really is a very optimistic person, in spite of how he looks. His undertakerish approach to personal expression gives the impression he's morose, but instead he's practically a mental health cheerleader, tugging away on his little devil goatee and adjusting the cuffs of his peg-leg pants over his pointy black boots. Lately I've really been giving him reason to hope. Just imagine if I brought home the crown. Then he'd really have something to cheer about!

March 17
Got the receipt for my virginity pledge today. They sent me a brochure listing the dates of various virginity conferences. Judging from the photos, my expectations of taking The Pledge and having it be a capital "E" experience weren't completely out of line. The virgins at those other conferences really looked like they were having a great time singing, clapping, being safely intimate with other virgins. And if I can get to Mobile, Alabama, for the next World Virgin Conference, I too can have a great time. No World Virgin events are planned for the Bulkley Valley in the near future.

I'm interested in the T-shirt that I could get with my pledge for a mere $25.95 extra, but I'm afraid to ask for my mom's credit card. She'd probably object to a T-shirt that reads "I'm Waiting—Ask Me What For!"

Since I'm not convinced this whole virginity thing is going to work out, I actually mailed the apology to Goose today. If I'm not going to remain a virgin until marriage, I want to be a nonvirgin with him. And I'd like him to be my date for the Sweetheart Ball.

All that's left is to wait for him to call back and make his own apologies after accepting mine.

THE FAMILY BUSINESS

March 18
As if my life needs more complication, my mother has decided that our candle business has grown beyond what she and her pieceworkers—my dad, me, and MacGregor—can handle. We're shipping our herb-scented beeswax taper candles all over northern B.C. and starting to get orders from Alberta. Who knew Albertans were into candles! She doesn't want to give up her job as assistant manager at the New Age/secondhand bookstore to devote herself full-time to candles. I don't know why not. I suspect she has an ego attachment to it. All the other New Agers treat her like an expert in everything from past-life regression to the latest and most bizarre bodywork technique just because she works there.

In her social set being well versed in the latest New Age scam is considered something to brag about. Also we're more or less living on that income.

She's going to hire someone from outside the family to do "order fulfillment" and "candle consulting." She agreed with me that MacGregor and I can't work any more than we currently do or it will interfere with our schoolwork. I put in only about fifteen minutes a week, but even that is taking a toll on my academic performance. And MacGregor really is genuinely busy. I get away with not helping much because I'm hard on the molds. They cost quite a bit of money and I dent practically every one I touch, so we can't get the candles out. We have about six boxes full of deformed candles that my dad has had to pry out of dented molds. He refers to them as Alice's Forceps Casualties. I don't know what he's talking about, but it certainly doesn't sound pleasant.

Anyway, the lucky candle employee will work in the basement with my dad. I'm hoping it will be a bit like having a servant. This family could use some looking after. We all get to sit in on the interviews and have our say about the newest member of the "team." I would wear my leather pants for the occasion, but I don't want to give applicants false expectations about family finances.

I hope my new commitment to the martial arts will help me to cope with all the challenges on the home front, in my professional life as a writer, and as an ambassador for the town of Smithers. Now that I have gone out for athletics in a big way, I'm more balanced generally. And my low blocks are really coming along. All that remains is to get my boyfriend back and I'm set.

March 20
The good thing about the Bonding Over Beauty event was that there was no talent involved, at least not on the part of the candidates. The official Miss Smithers chaperone, Mrs. Martin, took us to Star Snips Salon to get our hair done in preparation for the competition to go into full swing. I was a bit nervous, because I've had some bad experiences with haircuts in Smithers. My hairdresser (he prefers the term stylist) is located in Prince George. MacGee's Frolic is definitely the place to go if you want a cut that looks good in barrettes. MacGee himself is a hard-drinking Irishman who, if I was just ten years older and a man,

would be devastatingly attractive. Even though I am sixteen and a girl, I still find him pretty great. Unfortunately, Prince George is four hours away, and I can't get my mom to take me there unless she's recently done something awful to me and feels extremely guilty. You'd think that the 'zine incident would qualify, but Mother is still avoiding responsibility on that issue, saying that I should be grateful that she spends her time cleaning up after me when she could be out making the world a better place. We are going to have to be careful that Mother doesn't fall in with the wrong crowd, or we might lose her to the activist movement. I wouldn't be a bit surprised if one day my mom moved into a tree to prove some point. I admire people who have the courage of their convictions—I just hope they aren't neglecting their family responsibilities while they do it.

Anyway, the point is that I haven't had my hair cut in quite a while. You might call the situation on my head unruly or even out of control.

I watched the other girls go under the scissors, and it dawned on me that the one thing almost everyone else in the contest has in common is long, straight hair. How much damage could a stylist do to that? I could have cut those girls' hair. My hair, on the other hand, is quite complex, so when my turn came, I told the stylist I was growing it out but thanks very much anyway. The stylist suggested I might want to wait until the pageant is over. She said that the grow-out phase with a cut like mine could be quite "awkward." I said thanks, but I have quite a few barrettes. Mrs. Martin said, "Dear, a haircut would probably be a very good idea." And so I asked her what exactly she meant by that.

"Well, you are looking a little, ah, shaggy, I guess would be the word."

"I'm fine. Thank you. I'm growing it out."

The other candidates agreed.

"It looks good," they chimed.

"I'd just leave it."

"Definitely."

And so I just left it.

Those girls really aren't so bad after all. I might even bump up the scores for a couple more of them.

The beauty tips we shared afterward were interesting. Miss 4-H revealed the secret to her big biceps: twenty push-ups every night before bed—full military, not the girlie ones. Miss Evelyn Station Fish Hatchery recommended cucumber peels over the eyes for freshness.

"I try to stay away from fat and carbohydrates," said Miss Bulkley Valley Fall Fair.

"What does that leave?" asked Nancy, Miss Chicken Creek Fire Department.

"Oh you know, liquids mostly," replied Miss Fall Fair.

"For me it's all about the toenails," said Melinda, Miss Moricetown, in a rare shallow moment. "I put cotton balls between my toes and use cuticle lotion on them and everything."

It made sense. She spends so much time kicking people with her bare feet, her toes should look their best.

Miss Loggers' Association gave us a recipe to help ease hangovers, which Mrs. Martin tut-tutted but wrote down when no one was looking. Miss Panelboard Plant told us the name of a blemish concealer so thick "you could make a whole new nose out of it." I racked my brain and couldn't come up with anything. When my turn finally came, I blurted out the single word "deodorant," which did nothing to enhance my image with the other girls. Of course Esther had a seven-step skin "regime." Some people really have it all.

After we'd finished sharing beauty tips, Mrs. Martin took our measurements for the sponsors who were going to outfit us for the fashion show. She must be a lousy poker player if her reaction to our measurements was any indication. She had a gambling "tell" so big, she might as well have held up a sign.

She hummed while she worked, and when she took a good set of measurements, her hum became high-pitched with admiration. When the numbers weren't impressive, her hum turned low and mournful. In the worst cases it stopped entirely.

Afterward those awarded a high-pitched hum practically pranced out of Star Snips. Those of us given a low drone—or worse, silence—trudged out, heads lowered, sure we were going to get stuck modeling a one-size tent dress from Triple Stretch Sally's.

As I was leaving, Miss Bulkley Valley Fall Fair shot me a defensive look.

"She hummed. It was just quiet, that's all. It was near the end. She was getting tired. But she definitely hummed."

I didn't respond. I may be a writer in search of truth and honesty, but even I have a sense of decency. I'm not about to publish something as arbitrary and meaningless as someone's measurements in my 'zine. Unless, of course, I had the kind of numbers a person would want publicized.

Deep Inside Miss Smithers:
Part III

Things are heating up in this year's Miss Smithers Pageant (and we're not just referring to Miss Bulkley Valley Fall Fair's curling iron!). Some contestants are revealing deeper depths than anyone might have guessed. Others are facing setbacks with grace that belies their fashion sense. And still others are evidence that the old saying "can't judge a book by its cover" is not very accurate for a supposed truism.

So, without further *adieu*, the standings thus far in the contest!

(Please note that these scores are out of a possible ten and are not guaranteed to be scientific.)

Good going, girls! Way to improve those scores. Before you

know it, we'll know you all so
well, we'll be able to put your
real names on the chart!

—P. J. Hervey

COMPETITOR	BEAUTY	TALENT	CONGE-NIALITY	FASHION SENSE	COMMENTS
Miss 4-H	4	4	6	4	Candidate's moving up in the standings. Once you get to know her, you hardly notice her giant biceps.
Miss Northern Real Estate	4	3	3	4	Candidate's scores are steadily improving. What can I say? I'm in a good mood.
Miss Main Street	3	3	3	3	Amazingly, candidate has made it onto the chart. Is not as completely awful as her support group might indicate. Even seems a bit friendly, although sort of gruff for a 17-year-old girl.
Miss Panelboard Plant	4	3	2	4	Candidate has made progress, but only because she seems mostly harmless. Really needs to take her head out of her you know what and focus! Focus!
Miss Unschooling	3	3	3	3	Candidate has removed herself from the running. Her scores have been left up as a reminder to others. A sort of warning/memorial, if you will.

COMPETITOR	BEAUTY	TALENT	CONGE-NIALITY	FASHION SENSE	COMMENTS
Miss Deschooling	5	3	5	3	Candidate making slow but steady progress. Is apparently one of those quiet courageous types. Speaks only infrequently, but when she does, it's not completely incoherent. Unlike some other people I might mention who don't eat any fat or carbs.
Miss Loggers' Association	3	3	5	3	Candidate really very nice, but I think her parents should start saving up now for what looks like a much-needed trip to a treatment center.
Miss Ski Smithers	7	7	7	7	Candidate's perfection shows no signs of abating. Really, a terrific girl. But she, like all of us, has her own burdens to bear. Not that I'm saying her sister would be hard to deal with or anything.

COMPETITOR	BEAUTY	TALENT	CONGE-NIALITY	FASHION SENSE	COMMENTS
Miss Forest Products	4	4	4	4	Candidate still needs to work on standing out. Smoking a different brand of cigarettes than anyone else when the judges aren't watching isn't enough.
Miss Frontage Road	1	1	1	1	Thankfully, candidate seems to have retired hideous green sweater. Still, her cliquey ways are not at all nice. But I'm not feeling as resentful as usual: contestant makes it on the chart.
Miss Evelyn Station Fish Hatchery	5	4	4	4	Candidate's technique for applying eye shadow is fairly interesting.
Miss Chicken Creek Fire Department	6	6	6	6	A very nice person. Funny and unpretentious. That may not count for much in the world at large, but we acknowledge the value of such things in this publication.

COMPETITOR	BEAUTY	TALENT	CONGE-NIALITY	FASHION SENSE	COMMENTS
Miss Bulkley Valley Fall Fair	4	4	3	4	Candidate's sucking-up skills are advanced. A career in politics may be in her future. For that reason she has moved up in the standings, as she will likely be in a position to do us harm at a later date.
Miss Rod & Gun Club	3	3	3	3	A good writer. Also relatively good at blocking a punch.
Miss Moricetown	6	6	7	6	Fit. Has excellent-looking boyfriend. (Not that that matters. Funny-looking ones are okay too.) May just be a contender.

March 21

I am a busy person and can't always make people's feelings my number-one concern. How can I be expected to switch from being a journalist/contestant to being an employment agency in the blink of an eye? It's hard to believe so many people want jobs. So far I've taken seven messages from potential applicants for the candle job. Before I'd even gotten a phone number, one applicant told me there was "nothing funny about being out of work." So much for my small talk with the menials. All I did was ask him if he was currently employed. When he said he wasn't, I made a little joke about unemployment insurance and how he'd have to stay long enough to qualify. I guess it was a sore spot, because he told me to piss off. He said we could keep our job and that he wasn't going to be a nanny to "no snot-nosed kid," that obviously this "wasn't no proper manufacturing job" that would let a "goddamn dimwit" like me answer the phone.

I was quite taken aback. I was only improvising a little on the script my father left us. My father, as executive assistant to my CEO mother, has done up a script for taking calls from candle-making applicants. You might get the idea from this that my dad's incredibly organized and hardworking, but far as I can tell, the forms are just a plot to get us to do half the interview *and* weed out the unstables. I mean seriously, the minute people realize they're speaking to an under-twenty-one, they let loose with their terrible personalities. Like Mr. Hypersensitivity. I suppose I shouldn't have said that bit about "We don't tolerate slackers, sir, no matter what your background as a seasonal worker," but he was my first message and I wanted to try some things out. After he blew up, I felt sort of bad, so I star-sixty-nined him and had MacGregor call him back after he'd had a few minutes to cool off. MacGregor apologized and rebooked the interview, and I made a notation next to his name not to bring up his spotty work history.

I stuck very closely to the script after that. No more attempts at idle chitchat.

MacGregor took a message from a guy who wants to try out for my father's band. His name is listed simply as Murphy. I'm not interested in my dad's band or anything, but I did happen to look over Murphy's form, and it turns out that his musical influences are Flatt and Scruggs, The Pogues, and The Replacements. Naturally I was impressed since

I've never heard of those bands. The rest of my dad's group (Lyle and Matt) have influences as diverse as The Who and The Rolling Stones. Yawn. I think I will sit in on Mr. Murphy's interview. I might just learn something.

I have been working hard on my walk and pivot for the fashion show. I think I've conquered my tendency to trip at moments of peak stress. My mother hasn't been very helpful.

"Alice, could you please stop pacing. This is about the fortieth time you've been through the kitchen."

I wheeled around again with an elegant economy of motion that was completely lost on her and strutted back into the living room.

"Well?" I asked MacGregor, who was sitting in the recliner with a pad of paper and a marker.

He thought for a moment, marked something on his scorecard, and held it up.

"Seven?" I couldn't keep the disappointment out of my voice.

"You were walking too fast."

My dad, prone on the couch, nodded in agreement. "You have to slow it down."

My mother thinks it's just pacing. Ha! It's more

like an Olympic sport. Or an art. Or something. It takes my mind off waiting for Goose to call.

March 22
The thing about becoming a busy, not entirely unsuccessful person, with hobbies and activities and whatnot, is that one has less time to write. Look at me, for example. I used to turn out quite a few articles, and they were long, too. But now I am so caught up in living that I am having trouble cranking out ten words per day. Today's piece, "The Art of the Low Block," was only four lines long. It's a good thing I am my own publisher, or I might have to put some standards in place. As it is, I really should start thinking about when I'm going to release the explosive second issue of my 'zine. I hope I don't have to do all the work myself this time.

Speaking of which, no word yet from Goose. He should have my letter by now. What if he's found a new girlfriend? One who is normal? And what if her parents give her a bit of personal space and she and Goose are doing IT? It's too awful to think about. I'm starting to wish I'd been more apologetic in my letter.

To further complicate things on the romantic front, there has also been some indication that Jeff is interested in me. He has taken to walking me home from practice and giving me not very subtle suggestions for ways I could look better and begin to fit in. Last week he asked if I ever thought about wearing "nice" clothes. This week he questioned whether I could switch from the Alternative to the "normal" school. This indicates to me that he is feeling conflicted because he sort of likes me but wishes I was more popular or acceptable or something. I don't know why he cares. After all, he's already graduated and has that terrific job as a carpet layer's assistant. I appreciate his interest, I really do, but the truth is that I'm not about to go changing for someone I'm not that attracted to. Now if Mr. Teresa or Shawn asked me to be different, I might think about it, even though they aren't funny-looking. What makes them so cool is that they would never notice me enough to consider asking me to change. I mean, Mr. Teresa might suggest I do more good deeds, and Shawn might suggest I stretch more or something, but that's about it. And like I said, Goose for some bizarre reason seemed to like me the way I was.

Oh well, George may have done IT, but at least now I know I could too, probably. If I wanted. Which I don't.

March 24

Tonight after practice Jeff invited me to a dojo party for the Bears. No Bees or Butterflies are allowed. We are going to watch something called UFC videos. They have a 16+ rating, which is why the little kids can't come. It was probably quite a big step for Jeff to invite me, considering I haven't done a single one of his suggested improvements on myself. When he asked me to come, he said I was old enough to attend, even if I wasn't good enough. Then he hurried to explain that he just meant I wasn't advanced enough. Shawn rescued him by saying, "It's April twelfth at seven thirty at the Hudson's Bay Trailer Court, number thirty-two. Everybody over sixteen is invited." Then he shook his head at Jeff and walked away.

Between Jeff walking me home after class and offering ways for me to become more attractive, waiting for Goose to call to accept my apology, and practicing my self-confident stride for the upcoming fashion show, I am really quite busy. *Est la vie*, as they say.

March 25

We have an employee. My mother insists that Crystalline Clarity Focus Candle Co. has an employee and I am not supposed to get any ideas about fobbing off my chores on him. Mr. Polaski is an unemployed mill worker and, as my dad says, a "genuine character."

If my mom'd had her way, we would've hired one of the many hippie girls with a background in candles who applied, but Dad found in his question period that none of them had ever held a job longer than three months. One actually let it slip that she was headed to a Global Trade Protester seminar in Oregon two weeks after she was supposed to start. Upon questioning she admitted that she was just going to use us to cover fees and travel expenses. My mother found that inspiring, but my father got outraged in the way that only those people who don't work do at the thought that work might not be everyone else's top priority either.

Unlike the candle-experienced girls, Mr. Polaski has been gainfully employed since before time began, practically. He was at the mill for fifteen years. Before that he'd been "in the bush." He now does freelance construction on garden sheds and chicken coops but is "in the market for something steady-like."

Mr. Polaski is, as my dad said reverently, a worker. But I think the reason we hired him is that he is also a one-liner king. When asked about his wife, Mr. Polaski harrumphed, slid his thumbs under his thick red suspenders, and said something about her having to take her car to the mechanic's.

"Car problems?" asked my dad.

"She smashed the bastard up again last week. Ah, she's a good woman, but she couldn't drive a pig down an irrigation ditch."

My father gave a short, unbelieving yelp, which he covered with his hand. Mr. Polaski just sat immobile, hands on woolen work-panted knees.

Of course my father had to try and get Mr. Polaski to come out with another one.

Soon we'd learned that the "goddamn suit" who'd laid him off at the mill had his mouth "puckered up tighter'n a eagle's ass in a power dive" and was so incompetent he "probably couldn't find his own arse with a compass and both hands." That one made my dad cry. And so Mr. Polaski was hired. At least as far as my dad was concerned. My mother still had to be talked into it. She felt that one of the hippie girls would be a "better fit," due to their experience making and using candles. Mother's concerns may have stemmed from the fact that when she handed Mr. Polaski the four-page candle-making sheets and the admittedly baffling mission statement for the company—"To make and sell candles that keep users in the light of perception"—he held the pages away from him like she'd just handed over a pair of unwashed underwear. Sounding wary, he said, "This better not be one a them goddamn deals you gotta be a Philadelphia lawyer to understand."

"Wonderful!" breathed my dad as Mr. Polaski drove away. Then he headed inside to convince my mom.

STILL MAD AFTER ALL THIS TIME

March 28
Goose finally called. I was shocked to discover that he's still mad.

"You know, Alice, you were really rude."

I was so surprised, I almost didn't know what to say. Finally I came up with, "But I wrote you an apology letter."

"You blamed me, Alice. That's not an apology."

"I said sorry."

"No you didn't. You said you were ready to forgive me for ruining your life."

"Well, that's what I meant."

"Alice, what I did was a mistake. What you said to me wasn't."

I fought down the urge to argue with him. I was sort of impressed he was being so tough. It showed a lot of self-esteem.

"You're not the only one," he continued.

"The only one who what?"

My parents, omnipresent as air, walked in and out of the room, listening to my side of the conversation.

"Who, you know, worries about stuff," he said.

I decided to go for it. To hell with my parents and their big ears.

"Okay, then. I'm sorry. I miss you."

I could hear him breathing on the other end of the phone.

"Look, I miss you too. But if you think I'm, like, some pathetic loser, who can't ever get anything right . . . Well, I mean, I can see how you'd think that. But it's not how I want my, you know, girlfriend to see me."

"It's not true though. I don't see you like that. You get stuff right. The important stuff."

"I don't know, Alice. I just need to think about

231

things for a while. I didn't hear from you for over a month."

"But I said I was sorry." I was pleading and everything. It felt like I was hanging by my fingertips, scary but sort of exciting.

"Just let me think about things, okay? I'll call you," he said. And then he hung up.

The mutual apology conversation didn't go at all as planned. It was not at all what I needed heading into the most intensive time in the Miss Smithers Pageant.

March 29

If there were an award for most misfortune visited on a single candidate, I'd probably get it. My mother is leaving us. She was so inspired by the protesting candle girls that she is going off to an activist training camp next week for an anticapitalism holiday. She refuses to say where the camp is exactly, as though she has become not only an activist but also an undercover spy. Luckily, she's going to leave a phone number.

I can't believe that my mother's so dissatisfied with her life with my father that she is willing to leave at a moment's notice. She told me not to be dramatic, that she is only going for a few weeks and she has holidays coming to her at the bookstore anyway. Sure. That's what they all say. Next thing you know, we'll be visiting her at her new home in Cuba.

Things were getting a bit tense, what with me and Dad so upset and everything. Then MacGregor spoke up.

"It's okay, Mom. I'll look after things."

Dad and I looked at each other, embarrassed at being shown up again. It's not like Mac was trying to make us look bad. Any semifunctional person would. But my brother is eleven years old. I'm the one who's practically an adult. I had to step up to the plate.

"No, no. It's okay, Mac. I'll handle things around here," I said, and Mother gave me a doubtful look.

Dad, shamed into action, also volunteered.

"All right, you two. Never mind. I can handle it. Obviously."

Mother's look of incredulity became more pronounced. Then she stepped forward and gave Mac a bear hug.

"I know, sweetie. You'll keep things together." Then she kissed him on the top of the head.

Dad and I didn't argue. It was probably true.

You should really have to have a license to have

kids. I bet they wouldn't have given Mom one if she'd told them she was going to abandon us as soon as her social conscience kicked in. She knows perfectly well that Dad is almost entirely helpless and Mac has that demanding homework and extracurricular schedule. And even though she hasn't been exactly supportive of my candidacy, at least she's been consistent. We're heading into a critical time in the pageant right now. I need her opposition to spur me on through sheer defiance. There's the fashion show on Thursday, and I'm already in a weakened state from Goose's unexpected attack. And now this. It's all a bit too much.

THE EENSY WEENSY BIKINI AND OTHER CRIMES AGAINST HUMANITY

April 1

You've got to wonder about any event held on April Fool's Day. But not even the date can explain the bizarre clothes and outright indignities inflicted on the candidates at the Miss Smithers Fashion Show.

First off, there weren't enough clothing-store sponsors to dress everybody, so the organizers included non-fashion specialist sponsors. The Emergency Services Store and Adams Outdoor and Industrial Outfitters donated outfits. So did the local sporting goods store. And our official dresser, the very literal-minded Mrs. Escher, standing in for Mrs. Martin, who was home with a migraine, insisted on trying to dress us in clothes that reflected our titles. Miss Frontage Road, apparently on the strength of the roadwork connection, was dressed as a flagperson. She modeled a reflective vest and oversize headlamp and carried a sign that read "Slow." When she walked the ramp, the lights were turned down and somebody trained a flashlight on her so the audience could see how well she shone in the dark.

Miss Evelyn Station Fish Hatchery was forced to walk the plank wearing chest waders, a fly-fishing vest, and wraparound sunglasses. Mrs. Escher, possibly the stupidest woman in the Western Hemisphere, instructed her to hold out a pair of kickboat flippers at the turn, as though they were some terrifically stylish accessory, and then toss them over her shoulder as she walked back. Miss Fish Hatchery looked like the Creature from the Black Lagoon scraping her way up and down the runway. The last insult came when Mrs. Escher sent her out for the finale wearing an inner tube.

"Look at that, would you," cried the announcer. "Miss Evelyn Station Fish Hatchery has on a state-of-the-art kickboat—it even has someplace to stash your beer!"

It was really almost beyond belief.

In light of all that I got off easy. I modeled a feed-store ensemble—cardboard-stiff blue jeans, checked shirt, straw hat. I looked like something you'd put out in a field to scare off birds. But it could have been worse. They could have put me in a bulletproof vest and a duck blind. Or wrapped me in a grain sack with baling twine, added a bow and arrow, and called it an outfit. Come to think of it, that wouldn't have been far off the hobbit outfit I wore for the first day of school, the outfit that helped make me the social disaster I am today. So I guess I should be grateful that I merely looked like a cast member who'd just walked off the set of a low-budget production of *The Wizard of Oz*.

All my catwalking practice at home paid off. I didn't stumble, even though the work boots they put me in were three sizes too big and about as flexible as a pair of bricks.

The most tragic part of the very pathetic event was what they did to Miss Deschooling. Excited by her measurements, and obviously not familiar with the fashion conservatism of the homeschooling movement, they put her in a bathing suit. And not just any bathing suit, either. It was a white string bikini crocheted by the Smithers Ladies' Auxiliary Society. Apparently the Ladies are looking to expand from doilies into swimwear.

Even for someone like Miss Main Street, who's not exactly known for her modesty, the suit would have been indecent. The back and front of the bottoms were the same size, and the so-called top was so tiny, one of the girls said it looked like two pasties tied together. I don't know what pasties are, but they sound pretty small. It was as though the Ladies' Auxiliary thought they'd been hired to outfit Cher for a tour called Mostly Naked. Poor, poor Miss Deschooling. This went way beyond wearing blusher.

When I left to walk the platform, an ashen Miss Deschooling was holding the bikini between her fingers as though willing it to grow. She was surrounded by several members of the Ladies' Auxiliary, who were admonishing her in twitters and squeaks to hurry up and put it on.

"Come on, dear! It's nearly your turn!" they cried, excited to see their minuscule handiwork onstage.

The rest of us couldn't resist taking turns peeking out from behind the curtain when Miss Deschooling took the stage. She shuffled out, wrapped in a large bath towel.

"And here's Miss Deschooling modeling . . . a bath towel," called the announcer.

Miss Deschooling flushed furious red, and looked, panic-stricken, back toward the announcer.

Backstage, the Auxiliary ladies began to chirp in alarm.

"It's not a bath towel. What's happening? Is she wearing it? How does it look?"

One of them threw caution to the winds and hurried out to whisper in the announcer's ear.

"Ah, it seems that Miss Deschooling is modeling not just a fabulous bath towel, heh, heh, but also a bathing suit crocheted"–he paused to listen to another whisper–"make that hand crocheted," he clarified. "Hand crocheted by the Ladies' Auxiliary. Let's hear it for these fine ladies. They do so much good in our community. Bake sales, pancake dinners, meat draws, and now bikinis."

The little Auxiliary woman beside him curtsied coyly and then made her way backstage again, to be greeted by her comrades.

"Did you see it, Mildred? Is she showing it?" the ladies wanted to know.

Miss Deschooling continued her shuffling walk down the runway, head down, clutching the towel.

"The bikini is, well folks, it's under the towel. But I'm sure it's very nice. Since the Ladies' Auxiliary made it. By hand. Crocheted it actually."

Mildred scurried back onstage to consult with the announcer again.

"Yes, well, apparently it's a white bikini. And again, I'd like to point out that it's been handmade, that's handmade, by the Ladies' Auxiliary."

Then the microphone picked up Mildred's querulous warble.

"Why isn't that girl showing our suit?"

Miss Deschooling froze. The audience murmured nervously.

Then Mildred spoke directly into the microphone.

"Dear, they can't see the suit if you don't take off the towel."

Miss Deschooling had gone from red to green. She was locked in place, halfway down the walkway. Then, as we watched, her head came up, her shoulders went back, and she abruptly dropped the towel, yanked it back up, clamped it around herself, turned, and fled backstage.

"That was quick," said the announcer. "But I think I saw it. Yes, I think I did."

One of the Auxiliary members who'd been standing beside us as we peered out at the stage said doubtfully, "I think Mildred may have made the junior miss size by accident."

The announcer continued. "Yes, it was, as reported, a white bikini. And I must say, from the, uh, brief glimpse I got, the Ladies' Auxiliary outdid themselves. Really, they just did a superb job on the, ah, outfit. Let's have a big hand, shall we, for Miss Deschooling and the Ladies' Auxiliary bikini: a small but important role in tonight's fashion show."

Miss Deschooling rushed into the changing room. Esther and Miss Main Street went after her, and the rest of us who had already been up followed and stood outside the door.

"Are you okay?" asked Esther.

"No." The word was followed by a loud wet sob.

"You looked great. Really."

"I feel so stupid," she wailed.

"You shouldn't. You looked amazing. There's nothing to be embarrassed about."

We all joined in, telling her how nice she looked and how she shouldn't feel bad.

"Took a lot of guts to wear that even under a towel," said Miss Main Street. "Especially when the rest of us were practically wearing parkas. You should be proud."

I made a note right then to increase Miss Main Street's scores, no matter who her friends and supporters were.

Finally, Miss Deschooling, whose name is Mary, came out of the bathroom. She was bundled up again in her customary long dress and cardigan and winter coat. Her clothes looked strange against the bright stage makeup they'd put us in. We crowded around in our weird outfits, models in a fashion freak show.

"Ladies!" called Mrs. Escher. "It's just about time for the big finale! Take your places."

"I can't wear that thing out there again," Mary said, holding back tears.

"You have to," said Mrs. Escher. "It's your outfit."

"No, she doesn't. Not if she doesn't want to," said Miss Main Street in a low, unmistakably threatening voice.

Mrs. Escher backed off.

Mary, eyes red, smiled gratefully. "Thanks."

As we walked out to take our final bow, the Auxiliary Ladies began to chirp indignantly again.

"But our suit! Where's our suit?"

"You wear the suit, you want it out there so bad," growled Miss Main Street.

Mildred fluttered in dismay.

"What? What is she talking about?"

One of her friends set her straight. "Mildred, the girl's embarrassed. The damn thing's too small. It's a junior miss. I told you."

We swept past them to take our bows, and I think I started to see what the point of the pageant is.

April 2

When I left for school, a few minutes after MacGregor, my mom and dad were having an argument. Dad was making a last-ditch effort to get her to stay.

"Diane, is this really the best time to go away?"

"When will it be a good time? This is really something I feel I need to do."

"Yeah, but look at the situation. Alice is in the Miss Smithers. MacGregor is in school. Don't these things concern you?"

"I know you can handle it."

"But is this really the best time? We're in a bit of a crisis here. I'm trying to get the old band together."

"You and I both know that it's always a crisis around here. And the band does not constitute a crisis. It's an opportunity."

"But food. What are we going to do about food?"

"Please. There's a cookbook on the counter, and I believe there's a grocery store somewhere downtown."

She was barely paying any attention to him because she was busy packing and trying to decide on what activism outfits to bring to the demonstrators' training camp.

Later

As I got home from school, my mom was leaving in a Ryder van with a group of women. I think I saw one of the candle-making applicants among them.

"'Bye, Alice! 'Bye, MacGregor!" she called merrily as they pulled away. One of the women threw us a clenched-fist revolutionary salute.

MacGregor and I watched until they were out of sight.

"Oh dear," said MacGregor.

He was right to be worried. My father's a mess. We found him sitting in the kitchen, hunched over, looking defeated.

"Dad, it's only a few weeks," I said.

He shook his head sadly. Then he reached for the Yellow Pages and asked whether I knew of a good place in town for vegetarian takeout.

A MUSICAL INTERLUDE

April 3

It took about seven minutes for the household to fall into chaos. It's a good thing Dad's schedule is so free, because when he has anything to do, he overplans, making list after list. Now that he's trying to be Mr. Primary Caretaker and Mr. Errand Runner for MacGregor and me, he can't make lists fast enough. Good thing for him I'm not one of those people who are involved in school activities and sports teams and have dozens of friends vying for their attention.

As it is, I've had to repeat the rest of the pageant schedule to him about forty times.

"And then there's the Sweetheart Ball. That's the final event."

"My God, are you serious? How are we going to fit all that in? Seriously. I thought you were mostly finished with this thing."

I shrugged. "What can I say? The pageant has a lot of events. It's not like you have to be involved."

"It's insane. It really is. How do other parents cope with this stuff? And Mac, tell me again about the science fair. That's this afternoon? Couldn't they give us a little more notice?"

"I think they told us in January. The notice is on the fridge," said Mac, standing with the fridge door open, searching in vain for something to eat other than old dessert tofu and a jar of eggless mayonnaise.

"Forget it," I told him. "It's a barren wasteland and we are going to starve."

"The fridge!" Dad was outraged. "Who reads the fridge? I don't know how we're going to fit all this in. You guys and your relentless bloody schedules. Something's got to give. I just can't keep up."

Sure enough, something did get missed. Dad double-booked himself. He forgot he was supposed to audition his potential band member this afternoon. The appointment conflicted with taking MacGregor to the science fair. You have to hand it to my father: He chose the science fair.

Dad asked me to call and reschedule Mr. Murphy's appointment. And I would have done it, but Dad wanted to rebook for a time when I would be at school. I decided I would just tell Mr. Murphy his appointment was canceled when he got to the house. That way I could meet him and maybe ask him about his musical influences or something. I looked them up on the Net and they are pretty interesting. It turns out that The Replacements were probably the most famous bar band in the world, and Flatt and Scruggs had something to do with that movie *Deliverance*: you know, the one where the hillbillies . . . well, you know. And The Pogues were the drunkest band in the history of the U.K. *and* had really bad teeth, which goes to show that poor looks and poor performance don't have to be a barrier to success.

Looking at Murphy's influences, I felt like the worst kind of poseur. Because the truth is that if I were left to my own devices, I'd probably be listening to teen queen music. Thank God I've got *Spin* magazine to tell me what's cool. I figured that me and

Mr. Murphy could sit down and have a talk about music like adults, like peers even.

Later

Don't ask me where I got the idea. I really don't know myself. Maybe the freedom from maternal guidance went to my head. Or maybe the demands of civic life just became too much. All I know is that I answered the call of the dark side today. And it was good.

There I was, Saturday afternoon, no Mom, no MacGregor, and no Dad to bother me. Sitting on the couch waiting for Murphy, I started to get nervous. Even wearing my leather pants didn't help. It occurred to me that maybe a little drink would help to take the edge off my anxiety.

Just a little nip, that's all I planned. I thought it might be sort of cool and strike the right note if I was having a cocktail when Mr. Murphy came to the door. Given his influences and all, I figured he would appreciate the gesture. After all, I can't be Miss Smithers every waking moment! I really do have a lot more edge than most of those girls, even if I haven't had sex.

So I went to the cupboard where my parents keep their liquor and poured myself a glass of gin.

I've seen enough drinking in my day to know that it wouldn't taste very good straight, so I put some ginger ale in it. Gin and ginger: I'm sure that's a well-known drink. It wasn't very good, but I persevered. I got myself settled in, and it occurred to me that with my leather pants (which were still new and creaky), carefully tangled hair, and gin and ginger in hand, I probably looked like a musician myself. Who knows, maybe Murphy would get the idea *I* was the band-leader with the gig to offer. He'd ask me to call him Murph. Then he'd audition for me! Or maybe he'd discover hidden talent in me, just from the way I was listening or tapping my foot or something, and ask me to be in a band with him. Now *that* would be a talent for the Miss Smithers! I bet none of the other girls would be in a band with a grown man.

But, as I imagine musicians often are, Murphy was late. And I was still nervous, so I kept nipping away at that gin and ginger without even realizing it. Next thing I knew, the glass was empty, and since I didn't look half so musical without it, I had to get up and get myself another drink. Not wanting to rouse the parental suspicion by cleaning them out of gin, I decided to switch. The orange-flavored liqueur and the coconut-flavored Malibu had a nice tropical taste. They were quite sweet, though, so I followed them with a glass of scotch, which is what serious people drink. I don't know what genius came up with that recipe. A mouthful of unleaded gas would have gone down smoother. I had to gulp quickly, holding my nose, to get it all down. I was just opening a tall can of Extra Old Stock beer to get the taste of scotch out of my mouth when the doorbell rang.

He was here! I had to go get the door. But my pants felt all sticky. There seemed to be orange liqueur all over one knee, and it was covered with paper-towel lint from where I'd tried to rub it off. In fact, my whole right leg was covered with paper-towel pieces that wouldn't come off my sticky leather pants.

My stomach and I lurched toward the door. I was careful to keep my beer can held high, so Mr. Murphy would be sure to notice it and think I was musical.

I opened the door and there he stood. The man of my dreams. The man of Young Christians' and Miss Smithers judges' nightmares. He was temptation itself, a lick of dark hair in one eye and bad intentions in the other.

He opened his mouth and said, "Hey, babe." (That memory may just be wishful thinking.)

"Hello—" I tried, finding to my surprise that someone had filled my mouth with quick-dry cement while I wasn't looking.

He gave a crooked smile.

"I'm here about the gig."

"Gig—" I said, only it sounded more like "glug." So far the conversation was not flowing. I took a deep drink of my beer to show him how rock-and-roll I was.

Murphy may or may not have been dancing around the doorway, but it wasn't his seeming ability to fade in and out and multiply into doubles and triples in front of my eyes that interested me. It was his pants. He had on leather pants like mine, only tighter. He had on a bright-blue shirt with red piping. And big black boots.

As if that wasn't enough, when I tried to call him Mr. Murphy, he held up a hand and said, "Call me Murph."

I guess it was too much for me, because I threw up at his feet.

Unfortunately, he noticed. He stepped back carefully and said "Whoa," but I think he said it in a fairly nonjudgmental way. My hearing was muffled by the purse I'd grabbed and put in front of my face in an effort to stem the tide. I have a vague recollection of being on my hands and knees over the toilet, but at some point I must've stopped barfing and joined him in the living room, because next thing I knew we were both in there, and we both had beers and were drinking them. I hadn't quite gotten around to telling him that his audition was canceled yet because we were having this incredibly interesting conversation, although I can't remember what it was about.

I dimly recall telling him how I am a devoted and fairly deadly martial artist who hopes to be moved up to the nine-to-thirteen-year-old Bee group soon. I believe I may have shown him a few blocks and possibly even a high kick, which would explain the plant and broken pot smashed all over the living room floor. I also have a sense that I may have sung him a few lines of "Sharp Dressed Man" by ZZ Top and told him how much I liked his pants. (I hope that one is a false memory.)

All that was quite exhausting, so I had to take a little rest on his knee, which is where I was when Mr. Polaski came upstairs.

I'd forgotten about Mr. Polaski, who has started working on Saturdays, probably just to make my dad feel like a slacker.

When Mr. Polaski saw me sitting on Murph's lap, the two of us laughing and waving our beers in the air, basically the picture of the wild musical lifestyle, he didn't waste any time.

"What in the piss ass hell is this? You! Missy! Where's your parents?" Mr. Polaski demanded.

I took another drink and said with as much dignity as I could muster, "My mother has run away with the environment. And my father is very kindly giving me some much-needed space to work on my talent."

Mr. Polaski snorted. "That thing you got under your arse don't look too talented to me."

It ended with Mr. Polaski seizing our liquor and me trying to assure Murph that he had the gig while Mr. Polaski bullied him out the door, flinging profanities after him.

Obviously I am in love. How could I not be? Murph has my destiny written all over him. Especially since Goose hates me now. My father and MacGregor aren't home yet. I can hear Mr. Polaski grumbling in the living room. Something about "not paying him enough to be a goddamn baby-sitter." He clearly has me mixed up with someone who can't look after herself. As soon as the room stops spinning and I regain my mobility, I plan to go and dismiss him.

MISS PANELBOARD'S INNIE

April 4

There's a reason rock-and-roll icons like Keith Richards look so worn. It's because the rock-and-roll lifestyle is very demanding and there is a high price to be paid for freedom.

An example of that high price would be the headache I had late yesterday afternoon when my dad woke me up.

"Alice! Alice! Get up now!"

He stood in the doorway and ranted that it had all gone "too far" and what the hell did I think I was doing.

Apparently Mr. Polaski told him about Murphy.

I am grounded and sentenced to two sessions a week with Bob instead of just one. I mentioned that I thought I might be coming down with something and should maybe stay home from the Miss Smithers Charity Curling Bonspiel today, but my dad said I deserved every bit of whatever I felt after the stunt I

253

pulled yesterday. Also, when he called my mother to tell her what was going on, she told him she thought she'd noticed a dip in the Bad Thoughts jar. He asked me if I was stealing to get booze and drugs, so I was forced to tell him about the meat-eating incident. I told him I was worried about MacGregor's iron levels, but he wasn't buying it.

After he finished listing my punishments, he went straight out and called my mother for yet another consultation. I heard him asking her where she kept her mad-cow and hoof-and-mouth literature, as well as her copy of a PETA guide to animal suffering so he could give me a talk about meat and its dangers. Then he asked her if she had any stats on teen alcoholism. I can't imagine my mom's getting much activism done with my dad calling her fifty times a day. I bet she's sorry she gave us the number.

Later

It's not just the hangover talking. The Miss Smithers Charity Curling Bonspiel really was the most pointless of the many, many pointless events that make up the Miss Smithers Pageant.

We were supposed to spend an afternoon with disadvantaged kids who wouldn't otherwise get to do something fun like curling. We were all going to wear hats and, according to Mrs. Martin, the event would be very "mediagenic" and get lots of press.

The first problem, other than the obvious one that I felt like something a dog had coughed up, was that the disadvantaged kids didn't want to curl with us. The organizers waited until the last minute to find some disadvantaged youth, and when they finally located a few hanging around outside the PetroCan gas station, the kids passed, saying they weren't into curling. The special needs kids they approached weren't any more receptive. Eventually the organizers and members of the curling club had to drag their own kids down to the event. I heard Mrs. Martin, who's looking a bit ragged these days, telling all this to the bartender at the curling club while ordering her third drink.

It was quite humiliating. My kid, who, like all the rest, had to wear a tag that said "I'm her Little Buddy!" with his name underneath, was disgusted with the proceedings and with me in particular. He kept complaining to his mother, who sat drinking rum and Cokes with Mrs. Martin by the sidelines, that if he had to do this stupid event, at least they could have put him with someone cool like Miss

Forest Products. All the Little Buddies wanted to be with Miss Forest Products and Miss Panelboard Plant, because they'd gotten their belly buttons pierced the day before and were making quite a production of it. To give the puncture wounds room to breathe, they both wore halter tops and low-cut jeans and talked loudly and vigorously about the pain whenever they had to bend over. They spent most of their time in close consultation with each other about whose navel stuck out more and the positions in which their "barbells" sat.

"Oh my God! Like yours sits way down, eh?"

"Cha. Total. It's because I have like an innie. You know."

"Total. Mine is sort of like more of an outie, eh?"

"Cha."

The Little Buddies, who for some reason were all boys, were unconcerned with the fact that, due to the metal protruding from their bellies, Miss Panelboard and Miss Forest Products were unable to bend over far enough to aim their rocks. All the boys really wanted was an opportunity to touch the girls' midriffs.

You would think that the rest of us would have been able to use the opportunity to play up our unpierced advantages, but due to the large, unwieldy hats topped with stuffed animals we were forced to wear, we weren't able to play much better than the navel gazers. I wore a moose hat, and that, combined with the nausea and headache, took quite a toll on my game.

The only media that showed up was a photographer from the *Interior News*. He took a picture of Miss Panelboard's and Miss Forest Products's bellies. Mrs. Martin was quite upset about that and said that people were going to get the wrong idea about the pageant. Then she sat down again to finish her drink. Esther and her Little Buddy won the event, thereby increasing what probably is an already substantial lead. It's very hard to know how to play this. Be the good girl who wins everything or the bad girl who gets all the attention? Being the nothing who gets nothing really doesn't seem like that great a strategy. I've been using that technique for the last sixteen years, and all it has gotten me is the chance to wear a moose hat in the Smithers Curling Club, being ignored and disdained by my boll weevil of a Little Buddy.

THE DAY DEPECHE MODE BLED

April 5

It turns out that Murph isn't quite as good-looking as I thought. He isn't quite as young, either. He was waiting for me after school today in the parking lot of the Civic Center to discuss the practice sessions I apparently set up with him when I was pretending to be a musician. He was on foot, very drunk, and I figure his thirtieth birthday is a dim memory at best. Not quite the rock-and-roll dreamboat I remembered.

When I first saw him standing in the parking lot across the street from the school, I wondered why someone in administration didn't do something about the obvious deviant loitering near school premises. "There's a lawsuit waiting to happen," I said to myself. So you can imagine my dismay when he crossed the street to meet me, skinny legs barely able to bend at the knee due to the constraining tightness of his pants.

"Babe—" he said. "It's me, Murph."

Oh my God.

I cast a quick glance around to make sure no one was around to see me talking to this denizen of the dark. Mr. Murphy obviously had no idea how awful he was. He made a move as though he was going to try and hug me, and I nearly fell over trying to get away.

"So babe—" he repeated. "We gonna rehearse today or what?"

All I wanted to rehearse was him going away and leaving me to my youthful virginity.

"Uh, I can't today. I've got to go home. I'll, ah, call you when, you know, it's time to practice."

After an intense struggle, which included grunting and various upper body contortions, he managed to pull a plastic flask out of his back pocket. He took a deep drink and offered me one.

"Let's go to my place and we can talk some more," he said, displaying teeth that ended just past his incisors on either side. Not only was Murphy old and underweight, he was also in need of dental work. My mind flashed back to sitting on his knee and I nearly screamed.

"My buddy's got a rottweiler bitch. Just had pups. I could get you one," he said.

I had to get away from him. I will never, ever drink again as long as I live.

"Look. I really have to go. I've got an appointment. Um, we can meet tomorrow. In the rec room at the Teen Center. At three thirty."

Bob can tell Murphy that there's no band. After all, Bob's been hired to keep me out of trouble, and it's high time he started doing his job.

Later

This day just went on and on, grinding my rock-and-roll spirit into dust. I can barely hold a pen to page for the purposes of personal revelation, much less journalistic exploration. I more or less told the story of the fraudulent band auditions to Bob, preparatory to asking him if he could set Murphy straight for me. Bob didn't take it well. He got quite judgmental and parental.

"You got drunk!? And sat on some stranger's knee! Why, Alice? We were making such progress."

I am beginning to wonder if Bob is graded on his counseling skills by my performance in life. He pulled it together by the end of the session, though.

"It's okay. No, really, I'm fine." He lifted his head out of his hands, shook a few aspirins from the jumbo bottle in his desk, dry-swallowed them, and smoothed back his dyed black hair.

"Really, it's okay. We're fine. This is only natural. You are experimenting. Absolutely natural. We'll get through this together."

He took a deep breath.

"What time will this Mr. Murphy be here?"

"I dunno. After school tomorrow."

"Okay then. That's fine."

I don't know what's so fine about it. Once again my identity and personal image are in tatters. Although I'm clearly in need of saving, Jesus doesn't seem to be having much success with me. My career in journalism can't justify elderly toothless boyfriends. I don't dare tell anyone from the dojo about my little flirtation with alcoholism. Shawn and the gang are clean livers. They'd be disgusted. And if the Miss Smithers judges somehow find out, all will be lost. I may be Scottish and therefore a bit wild, but shouldn't there be a downhill slide of some kind? Who starts at the very bottom?

April 6
Spent the day dreading my appointment with Bob and Murphy. I was feeling extremely vulnerable, so I wore

261

all my largest clothing. In fact, I had so many clothes on, my dad asked me if I was trying to sneak somebody else to school in my outfit. Ha ha. Very funny.

School was as scintillating as usual. It did absolutely nothing to take my mind off my troubles. When I got to the Teens in Transition Center, I could see right away that Bob had taken a different approach to the threat. He'd gone for the very-little-clothing look. He had on a too-small black Depeche Mode T-shirt and some sort of terrifying black tights. I think they were meant to suggest a certain familiarity with weight lifting, but instead they made him look like the lead dancer in a ballet about the life cycles of stick insects. His all-black ensemble ended in a pair of gleaming white runners, which did nothing to increase the intimidation factor.

He was pacing in front of the rec room radiating anxiety when I got there. I immediately felt better. There's only room for one person to panic in any situation.

When he saw me, he stopped tensing his arms, a vain attempt to get a muscle to show itself in one of his biceps.

"Alice. There you are. I was worried. You're late!"

It was three thirty-five. School got out five minutes ago. Clearly it had been a long five minutes for Bob. "Where is he? Where is the guy? Is he coming?"

Suddenly I was Miss Cool. "Oh, don't worry. He'll be here. Musicians are always late."

That didn't reassure Bob at all, and he resumed his fruitless flexing and pacing inside the rec room.

I didn't get to demonstrate any more of my sophisticated understanding of musical matters, because Murphy showed up with his guitar slung over his shoulder, reeking of beer.

"Hey, babe," he slurred.

Releasing himself from a full body flex, Bob stepped between us before Murphy could go in for a hug.

"Mr.–?" he inquired, knowing full well what Murphy's name was.

Murphy wiped his lips with his hand and tried to focus past Bob onto me.

"So, babe, you ready to rock?"

Bob's face took on a look of cartoon dismay.

"Ahem," he said. "Ahem."

Murphy slowly swung his head back to peer at Bob through bleary eyes.

"Yeah?"

"Maybe you aren't understanding me—" Bob began. Well, of course Murphy wasn't understanding him. Bob hadn't said anything yet. "—this *child* in whom you've evinced such *interest* is, well, she's a child. A *youth.*" Bob paused. *"Illegal."*

Murphy looked over to where I leaned against the wall, slumped under my layers.

"Bullshit. She's runnin' ads for musicians."

Bob switched to full condescension mode.

"Sorry, bub, but her father ran the ad."

Bub?

Murphy didn't appreciate Bob's attitude or his hard-boiled lingo.

"Who you supposed to be? What is this, man? A sting? Entrapment? I didn't know how old she was."

Bob, misreader of people that he is, pressed his point.

"Oh yeah. Well, maybe you should think of such things before you engage in such inappropriate behavior. We've got a name for people like you, you know. It's a long one. . . ."

"Who you calling a pedophile?" growled Murphy, who apparently wasn't as dumb as he looked. Bob's mouth snapped shut when he realized he'd gone too far.

"Well, I—" he spluttered.

And just like that, Murphy popped him one. A short jab to the nose. Blood bloomed down Bob's face, disappearing into his black T-shirt and washing red over the white faces of Depeche Mode.

Bob held his hands to his nose and we both watched Murphy, God's gift to bar bands and little girls, leave out the front door, guitar still slung over his shoulder.

And can anyone blame me for noticing, through my relief of course, that there was something quite romantic about the whole thing?

CHRISTIAN SOLDIER

April 11

Having given up my dreams of a career in music, I have more time for self-improvement, with an eye to possibly winning the Miss Smithers contest and achieving spiritual enlightenment. I am still suffering from lingering self-disgust over the Murphy episode, so I've set up a prayer area in the living room and stocked it with the chastity pamphlets given to me by the Young Christians. Some of the pamphlets are a bit scary, what with the hellfire and all. I keep those on the bottom. When I'm really feeling bad, I plan to bring them out to scare myself straight. In terms of religious goals, I'm not really sure what I'm going for, but I figure that enthusiasm is an important component of spiritual growth.

My study of the martial arts is also quite spiritual. Shawn makes us all meditate for a few minutes after our cooldown. He also asks us, even the littlest Butterflies, whether we are meditating at home after we practice. I always say yes, even though I've never practiced or meditated. I suspect he knows I'm lying, and that's why I still haven't been promoted from remedial work with Jeff. I feel that I'm ready to sting like a Bee and am annoyed by the holdup. I hope it's not just Jeff's Educating Alice syndrome that is holding me back.

Call me crazy, but meditation seems contrary to ass kicking somehow. Shawn says the most deadly person is the most conscious one. Well, obviously it helps to be awake, but I figure the most deadly person is the one with the hardest kicks. But what do I know? I'm not even a Bee yet.

I've been thinking that adding a bit of Christianity to my martial arts might just be the thing to push me over the hump, spiritually speaking. What would a Christian martial artist do? Juggle stakes and torture instruments? Drag large crosses from town to town? Did Jesus have a favorite athletic activity?

Maybe I should give the YCs another chance. They might see me as more of a project than an individual, but I'm used to that. After all, I've been going to the Teens in Transition (Not in Trouble) Center for years now. I'd like to avoid ending up in a church somewhere vowing to be celibate not just until I get married, but forever! Surely the YCs have more to offer in terms of spiritual growth than just not having sex.

On the home front I am pleased to report that we are now getting along just fine without my mother. Although for a supposedly New Age guy, my dad is useless in the kitchen. We've had mashed potatoes with lentils every night since she left. I showed him *The Moosewood Cookbook*, hoping for a little more variety, but he told me to be grateful for what was in front of me, that my poor mother probably isn't getting even mashed potatoes. I imagine starving Highlanders lived a bit like we do now.

April 12

I have been sincerely trying to meditate but am finding it quite boring. In fact, I think meditation may *cause* sinful thoughts. It seems like the minute I try to clear my mind and embrace the emptiness, I start thinking about very unspiritual things. Like what will happen if Goose ever forgives me, what Jeff will try next in terms of improving me, what it would be like to be Miss Smithers. I also have quite a few revenge fantasies aimed at various people. But mostly I think about boys. I know I should save this for a confessional professional, but sometimes I even think about Mr. Disgusto Murphy. In spite of how revolting he is, there is just something about the thought of him playing his guitar and everything that . . . Well, anyway. I chase out those thoughts the second they appear. I have memorized two prayers now that YC Mark gave to me. They are printed on a little card, which is handy. I bring them with me everywhere I go and repeat them until the bad thoughts go. Sometimes it takes up to twenty or thirty repetitions of each before I get control of myself. I pray so intently that I overheard my father tell my mother on the phone tonight, possibly in the hopes of getting her to come home, that he thinks I might have a calling.

I have a calling all right. But given the thoughts I've been having during meditation, I don't think it's to the church.

Because I need saving so badly, I went to another YC prayer meeting today. Mark is as good-looking as ever. He and Esther make a lovely couple. The other Young Christians—Pamela, Kristen, Amy, and Terence and the rest—were all doing great too.

Smiling, radiating health and inner peace, they welcomed me warmly.

"Alice! Super to see you!" they chimed.

I hadn't been to a meeting in weeks. I wasn't wearing my Jesus bracelet. Would anyone notice? Maybe offer some suggestions for salvation?

"Welcome," they said. "We're just praying for world peace here."

All I could think was: How about praying for me?

I am a mess. I don't fit in anywhere. I also don't stand out. I'm deeply troubled to the point of almost breaking my virginity with a toothless old musician. I've been dumped. My counselor is not skilled, my mother has jumped ship, my best friend is never available, and I stole money to get meat. I am one big cry for help. Couldn't these people see that? How could they pray for world peace when they can't even help me get any personal satisfaction?

But pray they did. No one asked how I was or where I'd been. It's fine to have a cause and everything, but a little individual attention would also be nice. Is it possible that I'm too special for Jesus? Maybe I'm just too impatient for Him.

Too Special for Jesus or Just Pressed for Time?

Sometimes when a person needs help, such as spiritual help and perhaps enlightenment, a person would like that help quickly, i.e., a person often doesn't want to sit through a bunch of bake sales and prayers and so forth before she gets some spiritual satisfaction.

One problem with religion in general and Christianity specifically is that it takes too long.

If I can watch TV or take drugs and feel better pretty much

instantly, how can religion compete? It can't!

So that's why people who are religious need to make an effort to personalize and speed up their services. Here's a suggestion: If someone comes to you seeking, like, personal solace, for instance, don't pray for world peace. Pray for the seeker. Talk to that seeker. Possibly tell that seeker that she's a terrific person and very good-looking. I'm sure that would have a more immediate effect than praying for world peace, which, let's face it, is a bit of a long shot.

Take a page from our modern society and try instant gratification. It works!

—P. J. Hervey

THE PLEASURES OF PLEASE

April 13

I went to the dojo party at Shawn's last night. Lucky for me my father is in such a funk, he's forgotten that I'm supposed to be grounded. Oh well. Going to Shawn's wasn't exactly a high-risk activity.

Shawn has his own place in the trailer park across the highway from the high school. He is beyond mature. He's got a welcome mat shaped like a boxing glove at his front door and every household amenity you could imagine, such as couches and chairs and a kitchen table.

I don't know how I thought he'd live. I guess with him being quite young and everything, I thought he'd live with his parents. It turns out he's been living on his own since he was sixteen! He made enough money teaching martial arts that he was able to buy his own trailer when he was just nineteen. And not only that, he also supports his twelve-year-old sister, Helen. I'll be nineteen in a few years and I don't even know how to cook yet. I have to tell you, seeing Shawn's level of responsibility is a motivator for me to start taking home economics more seriously.

Shawn's party was a welcome relief after that horrible house party I went to with Karen. In fact, Shawn's party was probably the best of the three I've been to. No one was drinking. Instead, they were all having health shakes and protein drinks and eating baked chips and low-fat pretzels and fresh fruit. Body fat is a serious issue for martial artists.

Shawn was a gracious host of few words. His sister, Helen, who is the top Bee, was there too. She has seen her share of UFC videos, and even though she's under sixteen, she wasn't about to be left out of this one. Shawn sat me across from Jeff, who immediately started trying to get my attention by squirming and shooting excess energy sparks out the top of his head, at least until Miss Moricetown, or Melinda, as she's known around the dojo, who was sitting next to him, told him to sit still and gave him a fond but firm noogie on the top of his head. She even softened up enough to smile at me when I came in, and rolled her eyes at Jeff, which made me feel much better. I think Miss M. may have something going on with

Shawn, but I'm not sure. It makes sense that he would pick the toughest woman in the dojo if he was going to be attracted to anyone.

There was still a hierarchical feeling in the group. The Bears asked Shawn questions and he answered them. It was almost like what I imagine a Q & A session with a priest would be like. The students are a mixed bag of neckless guys and regular girls, some of whom are surprisingly small, but all of whom are very sincere and focused on health, kicking ass, and listening to Shawn.

Everyone had questions for him. Who is the best mixed martial artist in the world? If you could train at any club in the world, which would it be? What is the best meal for after a workout? Have you ever gotten out of an arm bar? Each of Shawn's answers eventually came around to the idea of personal discipline, controlling oneself, and working hard.

Several people told rollicking stories about abdominal exercises that everyone but me seemed to think were very funny, and then Shawn put on the first UFC video.

UFC stands for Ultimate Fighting Championship. I nearly panicked when the tape came on and I realized I was about to watch a sporting event that was banned in half the world. No wonder the Butterflies and the Bees hadn't been invited. I was probably going to see people get killed! Eyes gouged! Rings coated with blood! I averted my eyes when the half-naked girl carrying the card for the first fight pranced around the ring. Jeff nearly dislocated his eyeballs trying to get my attention then, so I was forced to look back at the screen.

Two well-muscled men stood in the middle of the ring. A large referee-type person shouted, "Let's get it on!" and they began to circle one another. A foot shot out. *Whap!* It made contact. Another kick: *Whap!* And then the two men were on the floor and things slowed considerably. Seminaked, they lay at cross-purposes. One had a hold of his opponent's arm, the other had a grip on a leg. They inched into position. And I do mean inched. The Bears, though, were riveted. They yelled out things like "Oh man! Did you see that? That's a Gracie move!" and "Oh, he's going for it! He's going for it!" I, on the other hand, could see no action on-screen whatsoever. After what seemed like a very long time, one of the combatants tapped the mat, the fighters stood up and shook hands, and the winner was announced and had his arm held over his head by the ref. The first match was over. The trailer erupted into shouts of exultation.

This was the sport banned in half the world? While they're at it, they better crack down on turtle racing.

By the second match I learned to listen closely to the announcers' commentary. That's where the action was. I discovered that the blond man in the second match was a street fighter-jujitsu specialist from Venice Beach. He had incredible strength and was undefeated in his last seven starts. His opponent was from the Gonzales family out of Puerto Rico. Gonzales was a Greco-Roman fighter with kickboxing tendencies. He was nearing the end of his competitive career, and this would be one of his last fights. He was trying to build up the Gonzales name and their fighting school, The Tiger's Lair, so this was an important bout for him.

As you might imagine, given those circumstances, there was a lot more drama in the second fight than in the first. Family honor. Age faces youth! If I paid very close attention, I could even see some of the moves that the announcers and the Bears exclaimed over.

After some rolling around on the floor, the

blond guy emerged victorious, although I'm not sure why. His teammates, who also looked to be street fighters from Venice Beach, handed him a T-shirt that he held up to the camera. It read, *I just did you up the %$*#!* The Bears agreed that the gesture lacked class and brought shame on the sport.

There were two UFC videos to be watched, with several fights on each, and by the middle of the second tape I was able to identify a good lock or arm bar. But all the protein shakes had filled me up, and I had to go down the hall to the bathroom. When I headed back to the living room down the narrow hallway, a hand pulled me into the bedroom.

It was Jeff.

"Alice?" he asked.

"Yeah?" I put sort of a pissed-off spin on it to try to put an end to the conversation before it began.

"Can I talk to you for a second?"

"Now?" I looked around. We were crowded into Helen's tiny bedroom. I must say, her decorating scheme was a schmozzle and not at all feminine. She had a signed Canucks jersey over her bed, photos of martial artists pinned up all over the walls. A large portrait of Shawn receiving his black belt stood on her desk, and Beanie babies peeked out from their hiding places in her bed, on the floor, and on her shelves. The door was covered in a large poster of Lil' Kim.

"Alice. Seriously. I wanted to talk to you."

I sighed. "Look, Jeff, I appreciate your, um, help, but, well . . ."

"You are a beautiful woman, Alice."

I nearly choked. "Are you drunk? I am not."

"Well, I've decided you are to me. No matter how you look."

I glared at him.

"You know what I mean, no matter how you are."

I just shook my head.

"Will you go out with me? Please?"

A note of something like pleading had entered his voice, and I couldn't decide how to react. It was awful. I hated it. But I liked it. The word please, I mean.

"Okay," I said.

Before I could clarify that okay wasn't what I meant at all, Helen appeared in the doorway to her room.

"What are you doing in my room?"

"Hi, Helen. I just had to ask her something. We're on our way out."

She frowned as we left, shaking her head in disapproval. I was flushed with shame and could barely make myself walk back into the living room. Would anyone be able to tell that I'd said okay? And what the hell had I said okay to anyway? I prayed Melinda wouldn't notice Jeff following me back into the room.

When the video ended, one of the guys with a car offered everyone who needed one a ride home. I immediately took his offer and got in the car, pretending not to hear Jeff when he said, "I'll walk you home," in his "please" voice.

That's where we left it. I have unplugged our phone. If I can avoid Jeff for a while, maybe he'll forget about me.

April 17
Close call after school yesterday. As I left the Alternative portable, which sits just over from the regular school, I saw a muscular person leaning against the wall outside. Jeff! He should be off laying carpet somewhere, or perfecting his right hook, but here he was practically stalking me!

I took a very un-Scots approach and ran away. I ran outside, across the track, and over the fence at the far end of the school grounds. Then I scrambled through the bushes and shrubs to the highway and took the long way home.

Not bad evasive action, if I do say so. Must be my martial arts training.

Just in case I wasn't already feeling hunted enough, another large bundle of chastity literature has arrived. No wonder those people don't have sex. They are so busy sending out virgin lit that they don't have time. This package had a list of events in Canada, mostly located in Alberta, which is problematic for me due to the Rockies and my mother's refusal to go into Alberta until they recognize the special health care rights of witches and midwives. How is a person ever supposed to achieve normalcy given such an upbringing?

Oh well, I need to prepare for my Miss Smithers speech. I would like to bounce it off someone, but my dad is too distracted by the demands of being a single parent. And MacGregor is brilliant and everything, but he's only eleven.

Lately I've found myself missing my mother a little bit. Even if we didn't always agree about things, she was a pretty good listener. And there was no doubt whose side she was on. She's been gone for over two weeks now, and already I'm having trouble remembering her face, which is basically quite tragic. I've even written an article about it.

When Good Parents Go

It's a sad and terrible thing when parents leave behind their responsibilities to pursue their own selfish interests. Sure, it's not as bad if they are complete bums and abusive and everything. In that case it's sort of a relief.

But if a parent sets up an expectation of being-there-ness— you know, if she drives you around and cooks a few meals, etc.—a child ends up being somewhat dependent. Although not totally dependent, of course, because that's not cool.

Which is not to say that the child in question would actually miss the absent parent. We're

talking about finding it more of
an inconvenience, really.

So in conclusion, if parents
are going to disappear, they
should probably leave behind nan-
nies and other service providers
for their dependents. Due to
expectations that they've set up.
Which is unfair.

—P. J. Hervey

Possibly not my strongest effort. I had a little
trouble with the thesis. But I really have to wonder
whether, when God's writing up that final report
card, He gives more credit to those who help
strangers or those who support their families. I think
the Scots way is probably to focus on clan, which
suggests that maybe my dad is right, and my mom's
family probably were English.

I miss Goose.

HARVARD, PRINCETON, AND OTHER LIES

April 21

Today I realized that a person can never create a new future for herself. She is basically at the mercy of the fates and her particular heredity.

Finn took me to the Mother-Daughter Tea and Speeches today. Even if she'd been here, my mother wouldn't have gone. She wouldn't have felt right breaking bread with any parents who would encourage their daughters in such a useless, sexist pursuit. She envies her friends whose long-haired daughters accompany them to women's circles where they windmill their arms and twist their faces into grimaces before they settle down to the serious business of moving rocks and feathers and shells around a blanket and reading each other's tarot cards while listening to Enya.

I would have gone alone, but Finn felt that would make it look like I wasn't "grounded in the community." Good thing for me Finn doesn't have the attention span to hold a grudge for long. I think he has developed an unhealthy investment in my candidacy. My guess is that the other Rod & Gunners have realized that he is completely incompetent outdoors and are having second thoughts about his membership. Well, truth be told, I think I may be having some qualms about wearing the Rod & Gun Club banner. The antihunting, -slaughterhouse, and -feedlot exposés my father has been passing to me are starting to make me question my host organization. I'm torn. I really am.

But no one could say I didn't try. In a repeat of our trip to the Rod & Gun Club Finn gave me a dismayed once-over when I got in the car.

"What in God's name have you got on this time?"

I was wearing my purple suit. I attempted to disguise its old-person origins by making every detail of the outfit look as eighties as possible. I pinned up one side of my out-of-control hair and let the other side fall in my eyes in a classic New Wave style that I thought showed a certain sophistication. I wore a commanding piece of red costume jewelry around my neck. It was my mother's and she's had it since 1985. She said she never threw it out because she knew damn well it would never biodegrade. I had some trouble finding the right kind of shoes until I gave up the idea of shoes altogether and expanded the search into boots. I found the perfect pair of granny boots with slightly peeled-back heels in the back of my mother's closet. My research has revealed that, in the eighties, granny boots were considered very youthful looking. I even put on purple eye shadow to match the suit, and gold lipstick to match the metallic chain belt. I finished the outfit off by draping my best plaid scarf over my shoulders for ethnic confidence. It's not the MacLeod tartan per se, but is quite close in terms of the style.

When I showed my dad the outfit, he nodded vigorously and didn't say anything. MacGregor was also large-eyed with admiration. But Finn's not related, so he said what he thought. "So, did you kill the old girl to get her clothes or just tie her up and loot her closet?"

"Very funny," I said.

"Seriously. What is this? You got four hundred smacks to put yourself together. This little number must have cost, oh, all of about ten dollars."

It was remarkable. He was only off by five dollars.

The shoulder pads in the suit were so big, the left

one pressed into Finn's shoulder when I climbed into the passenger seat of his car.

"God," he complained, "those bloody things are a hazard. I can barely shift."

Then he groused, "Well, I hope you've at least got your speech prepared. With a getup like that, it better be good."

The first shock came as we pulled into the parking lot behind the Legion. Who pulled into the spot beside us but Miss Frontage Road, being driven by the late-fees-obsessed librarian! The librarian was Miss Frontage Road's mother! All became clear—it was a setup—I'd been framed! I reeled at the thought of Miss Frontage Road's mom deliberately sabotaging my campaign by spreading the 'zine far and wide. Any positive thoughts I'd been entertaining about the pageant and the contestants evaporated. This was a dog-eat-dog contest. Just like I thought.

Needless to say, due to the shock of the betrayal and the pressure of the event itself, plus the fact that the overlong bang I'd combed over my eye blocked half my vision, I was distracted during the tea. Finn had to do most of the talking for us.

At one point he elbowed me in the side and

hissed, "It wouldn't kill you to show a little goddamn vivaciousness, would it?"

I couldn't focus or even see that well really during the post-tea meet-and-greet with the judges. Finn made up for my silence though. He was like three dynamic mother-daughter teams all on his own, with his hand shaking, giggling, and whispered compliments to the judges on their clothes and hair. It was almost enough to make me miss my mother.

When it came time for the speeches, we all sat down again. I listened to the other girls, and it dawned on me that the speech I'd prepared was all wrong. I had written a short speech spelling out some of the problems with the Alpine theme on Main Street. Ever since I did that Mainer with Karen, I have considered myself something of an expert on the subject. One problem is that the large alpenhorn man at the entrance to Main Street is defaced practically every other night with toilet paper and other debris. Two is that the roundabout at the end of Main Street is hard for trucks with large tires to negotiate and is basically an accident waiting to happen. And three is that the interlocking cobblestone bricks may charm the tourists but, according to my sources, are not an ideal surface for people in high heels.

I thought my speech demonstrated me to be a critical thinker who cared about the town, but I realized that compared to the other girls my speech just sounded critical. Negative even.

Everyone was talking about their volunteer activities and civic affiliations and athletic participation. But I wasn't properly a part of any group. I couldn't even get promoted into the thirteen-year-old Bees. And I wasn't really affiliated with the shooters at all. I was like a backward ringer, brought in to help the Rod & Gun Club lose.

"I help collect toys for the Motorcycle Toy Run. I've been doing that with my dad since I was ten," said Miss Main Street.

"I've been a volunteer gymnastics teacher for seven years," said Miss Forest Products.

"I am active in band politics and promoting the culture of our people in traditional dances," said Melinda.

The crazy thing is, I think they were telling the truth. All those girls really did do good in the community. For free.

Everybody had something they did, something they believed in, something they were good at. Miss 4-H had 4-H. Miss Northern Real Estate volunteered at Habitat for Humanity. But I had nothing. I was just a miserable loner who hung out in thrift stores and criticized things and couldn't even get promoted in her dojo.

Somebody should have told me about the trend toward charity earlier. It seemed unfair to drop it on me now. Sure, I'd read in the *Utne Reader* about the growing spirit of volunteerism in North America, but who knew it had penetrated to Smithers? Isn't a person allowed to be self-centered until she's at least eighteen? Whatever happened to childhood?

Desperate times call for desperate measures. So when my turn came to speak, I improvised.

I got up in front of the judges and within moments found myself telling them that I hope to be a doctor when I grow up so I can join Doctors Without Borders. I repeated it in French too, *Doctors Sans Médicins*, in an effort to further impress the judges. Then I really started to lie.

I told the judges and assembled guests and candidates that I was working on my black belt in karate (joining the Bees just didn't sound quite right), and that I have been tapped to edit a prestigious journal of teen culture. I said I was an active and possibly even key player in saving the environment. I said I planned never to own a car. I said I thought Harvard and Princeton were both part of my educational plans, probably to be paid for by a Rhodes scholarship. I said that I was working on solutions to the problems of the wealth gap, as well as war and poverty everywhere. To sum up I gave an impassioned plea for the children that ended with the words: "Please give generously."

Silence greeted the end of my introductory speech. And then a lone voice coughed the word "bullshit" twice.

Who said it? The other girls stared at me, even the nice ones, faces frozen, long straight hair sitting perfectly on their heads, afraid to be caught sneering or laughing in uncandidatelike expressions of triumph. Everyone else's face was frozen too, revealing nothing. And Finn? A variety of expressions chased one another across his face. Amazement, dismay, anger all made appearances and then disappeared.

That heartwarming business with Mary at the fashion show was a lie and a fraud. These girls were all snakes. I couldn't decide which I hated more: them and their lies or me and mine.

I walked straight out of the Legion, past the rows of tables lined with eager candidates and their proper mothers and the lurking whisperer, whoever she was. My shredded granny boot heels clicked as I walked. I paused only once to catch my balance when a tea tray caught me by the hip on my blind side. Out the door and into the evening I went, leaving in my wake less competition for the other girls and audible evidence that I am not now, nor am I ever likely to be, a winner.

Finn followed me out and, when I wouldn't get in the car, drove slowly beside me until I finally agreed to accept a ride.

"Come on. It wasn't that bad," he said as I opened the door.

"Yes it was." I was sort of crying, half in anger, half in shame.

"A little embellished maybe. But you've got to exaggerate in these things. That's the way it's done."

He was so nice, it made me cry even harder. I was still crying when we got to our house and I jumped out of the car and ran into the house and into my bedroom.

I can't stand myself sometimes. Seriously. I feel almost like I might be allergic to myself.

My dad's checked on me about ten times since I got home, but I am not about to discuss it with him.

I'm sure he and Finn have already been over the whole sorry story in enough detail.

GIVING UP IS FUN TO DO

April 22
I've decided to quit the pageant.

I informed my dad when he came to check on me this morning.

"But it's almost over," he said.

"I don't care. I'm through."

He seemed strangely disappointed. "Well, okay. If you're sure. Have you told Finn?"

"I will."

"Well, okay then. If that's what you want."

That didn't feel nearly as satisfying as I thought it would.

Later
I appear to have lapsed into a feeling of unwellness. I'm not sure yet whether it is physical or mental. I suspect it's a combination of both. My dad called my mom to ask what to do, and she told him that I prob-

ably need to detox from my exposure to meat, alcohol, and organized sexism. She may be right. She prescribed some natural remedies for him to administer.

Later

I actually am sick. Am having feverish dreams of going hunting in my leather pants with the staff of Rotten Ryders and all the Miss Smithers candidates. We are running in a line and the deer are running in front of us. Goose and Jeff are behind us, and they are carrying guns. Jesus is watching and seems to be holding some kind of scorecard. Everyone but me remembered to wear their WWJD bracelet.

I may have to do that teenaged girl detox program. Anything is better than having another dream like that.

April 23

There is a good chance I am starving to death. Detoxification—ha! Starvation is more like it. Now my feverish dreams involve me sprinting after a giant bag of potato chips, but tripping in a field of carrots and other root vegetables. My dad, in a fit of paternal excess, has me pouring gallon after gallon of fresh vegetable and fruit juice down my gullet. I never thought I'd look forward to a small bowl of steamed Swiss chard covered in sesame seeds, but that day has arrived.

April 25
Washing out of life early is not that unusual. In the old days people also used to peak early. I'm able to pinpoint my high point, exactly. I just feel like a person can explore herself only so far to find almost nothing of interest before discouragement sets in. The way I see it, in the past little while, I have discovered that I am not:

1. Able to stand up to the demands of the admittedly not very fierce competition for the Miss Smithers crown.
2. Able to drink without exposing my lack of moral fiber.
3. Able to graduate into the nine-to-thirteen-year-old group in a mixed martial arts program.
4. Able to know God or hang out with the Young Christians without feeling like a sinful impostor.
5. Able to have fun sinning and eating meat without feeling guilty about it.

6. Able to appreciate the lifestyle choices of popular people.
7. Able to cope with the thought of having sex or not having sex.
8. Able to maintain even one friendship.

I could go on, but I remain too depressed to do much more than eat. Never mind success, functioning at all seems like an impossible dream for me at this stage.

I am lost and I can't get up.

Later

MacGregor's been trying to make me feel better. He just offered to get me junk food—a risky proposition in our house. He even brought in his latest naturalist acquisition to show me. It's a newt he's named Ned. Seems like just yesterday he was into guppies. How quickly they grow up.

Later

When Finn came over tonight, he poked his head into my room. He was probably checking to see if I'd actually died from humiliation. I guess my dad hadn't had a chance to tell him I'd dropped out.

He found me lying on my back in my flannel pajamas, a toque, and sunglasses, and staring at my oversize fuzzy slippers.

"How is our little Miss Smithers?" he asked.

I suddenly felt ashamed.

"I'm going to quit."

"You're what?"

"I just don't think it's working out. So I'm not going to finish."

"Now? You're quitting now?"

I shrugged and continued to study the ceiling. Finn, for once, seemed at a loss for words. He made a noise, somewhere between a sigh and a sneeze.

Then he gave up and continued down the hall. I heard him speaking to my dad and the words "had been doing so much better" and "finally found a few friends" and "actually getting out of the house now and then." Rather than listen to any more, I put on my headphones. Now I've managed to disappoint Finn, too.

April 26

My depression has been punctuated by more social activity than I've had before in my short lifetime. In an incident that made me feel like I might have a future on the Psychic Friends Network, several of the YCs stopped by after school today. They were very nice and concerned but had time only to drop off a few chastity pamphlets before, as Mark put it, arm around Esther, they had to "split to do good works." That's me: just another stop on the charity route.

But here's the thing. As they were leaving, Karen showed up. She brought me a *Harper's* magazine and her favorite book, *A Confederacy of Dunces*, which she assured me was not a dig at my intellect. She just thought I might enjoy it.

Karen stayed for almost an hour and was quite a fun visitor, telling me all about the goings-on in her life. When she left, she said she hoped she hadn't stayed too long. I told her I was glad to see her. With a funny, crooked look on her face, she said, "Hey, the more time I spend with you, the less time I have to spend with me. Least with you I don't have to get wasted just to stand the company." I couldn't help feeling that was a major difference between Karen and the YCs. She actually seemed to need me.

I practically felt better, at least until my dad delivered several messages from Jeff. One envelope contained a small plastic Yoda with a childishly printed note that said: "He gives good advice," and a

Luke Skywalker toy accompanied by a note that read: "May the force be with you." I was almost impressed. Jeff seemed like the kind of guy who'd give a person flowers or something. Toys are much more inventive. But I'm still not interested. Goose may be mad at me, but I plan to be available when he gets over it. I mean, who else am I going to find who makes me look neat and tidy by comparison?

Even Bob called this afternoon, saying he was sorry I wasn't going to make it to my appointment.

"Alice."

"Bob."

"What's new?"

"Not much."

"You're sick?"

"Pretty much."

"That's too bad."

For someone whose entire career depends on talking, Bob's a terrible conversationalist.

"So things are good then?" he continued.

"Fine."

"Alice, your dad called. Said you were quitting the Miss Smithers Pageant."

"That's right."

"Do you want to talk about it?"

"No."

"Well, if you change . . ."

"I'll let you know."

"Right. So . . . I hope you feel better soon."

"Thanks."

"See you next week?"

"Yup."

Click. That was it. Bob's don't give up, *carpe diem*, Dead Poets Society pep talk. I hope he never gets a job as a hostage negotiator. He's the least persuasive man.

April 27

As I had feared, I am mostly recovered, physically at least. But I am still suffering spiritually. When I said I still felt sick this morning, my dad went to check my mom's homeopathic books to see if he'd gotten the dosages right.

My mom is not one to doubt her own remedies, so I appreciate his thoroughness. Usually when she takes us to the regular doctor, he tells her that we've got the flu or a cold or something like that. Then he warns her that she should be careful with her alternative remedies, that they could be doing more harm than good. That always gives her a strong need for validation, so she immediately talks to her naturopath or some other alternative practitioner, who confirms that she is more or less a diagnostic genius and that her remedies are unusually insightful and potent. That's what I love about my mom: If the facts don't fit your theory, just find some new facts. Well, my dad's not quite as confident in his medical expertise, and frankly it's a relief.

The only problem with enjoying this last phase of my recovery is Mr. Polaski. He seems to have a nose for malingering. Every time he comes upstairs, I have to hide my snacks, books, and magazines and pretend to be asleep. Like a whiskery old gopher, Mr. Polaski's head pops out of the stairwell to sniff around about once every fifteen minutes. I can sense him staring at me lying on the couch. He hasn't caught me looking well yet, and I have begun to make it into a bit of a game. I switch positions between his little visits. One time I'll have my feet pointing at him, and the next I turn so my head is toward the stairwell. Ha! I bet that's messing him up. He's getting frustrated. I can tell from the grumbling noises he makes as he heads back down the stairs. Those of us who are creatively oriented find these people with a strong work ethic hard to take.

Part of the reason my dad lets me stay at home, even though I don't seem very sick, is that he's afraid to be alone with Mr. Polaski. My dad used to have the lifestyle of kings. He's a writer, after all. He rolled out of bed as late as possible (but before noon, because there are limits), drank his coffee very slowly, and then made his way downstairs to "write." I suppose he occasionally does write, but he won't show it to anyone and my investigations haven't revealed anything other than the bodice rippers he writes for the historically oriented soft-porn magazine out of Florida. He says writing the bodice ripper is an art; that it's all about understanding how large amounts of clothing can come off in the most provocative way.

After a couple of hours of "writing" he would make candles and help with shipping and invoicing, or at least organizing the work for MacGregor and me to do when we got home from school. But the worm has sure turned since Mr. Polaski got here.

Mr. P. shows up at the crack of dawn to begin work, and he gives my father looks of lethal disapproval when Dad finally emerges from the bedroom at eleven o'clock. This week I heard my father try to explain to Mr. P. how writers must have more "fluid" schedules, due to their need to think up creative thoughts, but Mr. Polaski wasn't buying it.

"You young buggers wouldn't know a day's work if it bit you on the arse."

My father couldn't even be pleased at being called young, because the rest of the comment was so negative. He tried to defend himself.

"Yes, you see, but I'm a writer. I have to spend time thinking and reading or I can't write."

Mr. Polaski gave a disgusted snort. "Useless, that book writing. Too much learning, not enough working. I only got my Grade Eight. Think it hurt me any?"

Dad retreats into himself a little further each time he gets hit with a blast of Mr. Polaski's semi-incoherent but deeply felt criticism. And every morning he gets up just a little earlier.

Finn, Marcus, and Kelly tried to have an afternoon visit with my dad the other day, but they got caught by Mr. Polaski. When my father had been upstairs for longer than his allotted bathroom time, Mr. Polaski emerged from the basement. When he saw the four Geniuses sitting around the table, his expression was like that of someone coming unexpectedly across a heavily illustrated case study of flesh-eating disease in their Lee Valley Tools catalogue.

Mr. Polaski asked my father if he was coming back to work.

Dad cleared his throat. "Ah, not just now. We're having a drink."

"I can see that," grunted Mr. Polaski.

He stood in the doorway and stared at my father's friends, who made a brave effort to continue their drinking but couldn't look at one another.

Finally Mr. Polaski could contain his disgust no longer.

"Don't you guys got no work to do?"

He jabbed a disdainful digit at my dad. "I know he's due for a break. He's been at it almost half an hour now. But there can't be four of youse with nothing to do in the middle of the day."

Marcus and Kelly looked downcast, but Finn bridled.

"We are having a business meeting here, sir. I don't know who you are exactly, but I'd imagine *you* have some work somewhere you should be doing."

My dad and the other two snuck small hopeful glances at one another.

I'm not even sure Mr. Polaski heard Finn's outburst. Instead he continued with his well-honed observations of life around our house.

"I never seen such a slack-ass operation in all my goddamn life. This one"—thumb stab at my dad—"he don't get outa bed till noon. And that one"—head jerked toward me—"wouldn't get off the couch if it was on fire. Except when she's getting into the booze. Then you should see the goddamn characters come crawling around this place."

Mr. Polaski snorted again. "All I know's I was hired to make them candles downstairs, and with all the carrying on around this outfit, I can't get a licka work done."

He sighed and shook his head. "I guess I'll just have to call and tell your missus it's not working out."

My dad started out of his chair. Mr. Polaski couldn't tell Mom! Mr. Polaski was my dad's employee, my dad's hire, his choice over the candle-experienced hippie girls. My dad was supposed to be supervising him in candle-making, not acting as an impediment to his overwhelming work ethic.

I bet those little hippies with candle experience are looking pretty good now.

THE ARGUMENT FOR STICKING

April 28

My sickbed has become one of the busiest places in town. Today I got visitors from the dojo. Shawn came by with Jeff and Melinda. He left me a copy of *Grappling* magazine and some protein powder and told me to hurry up and get better so I could come back to practice. Jeff, who looked gigantic and rudely healthy in the dim pallor of my messy room, and smelled of something carpet related, didn't seem to know what to say. When the others chatted, he stood well back. During a lull in the conversation he spoke up: "So hey–" he boomed, startling everyone. "How you doin'?" he asked, managing to lower his voice.

I'd already answered the question, and Shawn and Melinda looked at him.

Jeff pointed to the Yoda and Luke Skywalker toys on my bedside table.

"You like those?"

I nodded.

He pointed beside them to a bottle of homeopathic remedy.

"What's that?" he asked.

"It's a homeopathic," I replied.

Jeff looked confused.

"It works with your natural tendencies. To help cure you," I explained.

Jeff looked even more confused.

Then he nodded and looked at me carefully. "Oh, I get it."

Shawn and Melinda roared.

"It's medicine, man. What did you think?" Melinda laughed, punching Jeff in the arm. He rubbed the front of his ENTER THE DRAGON T-shirt and shook his head.

"Nothing. That's cool."

After they left, Melinda pushing Jeff in front of her, I only had a few minutes alone before my dad brought in yet another visitor.

Finn stood in the doorway.

"So what're you going to do for your talent?" he asked.

I stared up at him.

"I've decided that you can't quit. You came too close to finishing this thing to give up now."

I shook my head.

"Oh come on, Alice. Don't be a damn coward."

"They hate me," I said, trying to control my voice.

"Sweetheart, they don't hate you. They're just scared of you."

I struggled to get myself under control.

"I don't even care about the stupid pageant."

"Don't give me that. Your dad says you haven't been to school in a week."

"So?"

"So?" he replied. "So! You can't just quit life due to a couple of setbacks."

"I'll give your club back the money."

"They don't want the money. You know, when I was your age," he began. I waited for the big confession about his dashed beauty-pageant hopes.

"–If you want to know about not fitting in, sweetheart, just ask a gay kid from Brandon."

Lost in thought, he stopped for a moment.

"But the thing is, once you just decide who you are . . ."

Another pause.

"Ah, shit, what do I know? For what it's worth, the club's still behind you. A lass from good Scottish stock like you, you'll figure it out."

May 6

I've reached a decision. Since it means so much to Finn, I'm back in the Miss Smithers. I'm not going to let a few extremely embarrassing incidents or a couple of girls with crappy personalities ruin my life.

Unfortunately, I've lost a valuable week of preparation. The talent show isn't far away and I'm not ready. It's too bad I have no idea how to start. I'm sure I have talents. They just aren't recognizable as such.

It's probably a good thing I'm back in the contest. Mom's going to need something to oppose now that her career as a protestor has been cut short. She's coming home a week early because she got arrested for harassing some developer. She and her friends camped outside his offices and refused to leave until the police in Nanaimo apprehended her and the cement block she was chained to. Dad left for Vancouver Island this morning to spring her from jail. After he got the call, you've never seen a man move so quickly. He grabbed a sweater and his keys, and told me to look after Mac (then whispered "Just a formality" to Mac, as though I couldn't hear).

May 7
Today was a very big day. Goose called. He wants to get back together.

I, of course, played hard to get.

"Hi, Alice."

"Goose!"

"I've been thinking–"

I interrupted. "So? Am I forgiven?"

"I forgave you last time we talked. But I have to at least pretend to have some self-respect. A man's got his pride, you know."

I remembered all over again why I like him so much.

My parents got home this afternoon. My mom was surprisingly cheery for a felon. She said that she felt alive and connected. She also smelled overpoweringly of patchouli and pepper spray. My dad couldn't keep from staring at her with glazed-doughnut eyes. Really, they are quite a pair. Apparently they haven't given one thought to what I've been through lately. Oh well, it's good to have her back. I am ready for something other than mashed potatoes and lentils. I guess I'm even ready to go back to school.

May 10

When I returned to school, I got a nice "Welcome back" from the YCs. They have been busy planning a missionary trip to East Vancouver. They are supposed to get funding from their various churches, but unfortunately a couple of the biggest churches can't afford to donate due to needing to set money aside to settle pending lawsuits. The trip is looking precarious for all but the born-agains, who don't want to be selfish and go all by themselves to do good work in East Vancouver. It's a real problem and they are looking at a lot of car washes and bake sales in their future. So I guess the long and the short of it is that while the YCs were happy to see me, they were distracted by financial concerns. Esther and I had a good chat though, and she said she was glad I've decided to stay in the contest.

I didn't see Karen. I was afraid to look for her in case she was with her friends. They are so spinny that trying to talk to them is like getting too close to helicopter rotors going full tilt: windy and confusing. Unless they're sober, of course, in which case they're so burdened with the weight of being cool and popular that they can barely spare a glance, much less a word.

Throughout the day I ran into other Miss Smithers candidates, most of whom said hi and asked how I was. No one mentioned my performance at the speeches. Was I wrong about what happened that afternoon? Maybe not all the candidates rejoiced in my failure? I'd hate to think my perception was *that* warped. Oh well, if nothing else, this contest seems to have quadrupled my list of friends and acquaintances.

Strangely, everyone in my family is very excited that I am back in the contest. Even my mother has abandoned her antisexist stance in the face of kinship-based competitive blood lust. Possibly her activism has refocused her aggression. The home front has been a happier place since she got back. Dad has a skip in his step, and MacGregor looks less worried. I guess even I'm okay with it. Although, obviously, I'm not as dependent on her as they are.

The whole family has been brainstorming talent ideas. Dad thought I should do an exhibition game of Scrabble, but he was getting me confused with MacGregor, who is actually good at Scrabble. Mom thought I should write an essay and read it out loud. I pointed out that that would be a lot like doing a speech, and God knows I've already done one of those. Finn suggested I sing. He cut short what he was saying when he saw my mom and dad shaking their heads a little desperately. I may be tone deaf, but that's no reason to be unpleasant.

Like Finn said, I'll figure it out.

I asked Goose on the phone what he thought I should do, and he said, but not in a self-pitying way, that he wasn't exactly the right guy to ask about talent. Then he said he'd give it some thought. And he will, too. Because he's that kind of guy. He may not be entirely competent in the standard areas, such as sports and mechanics, but when it comes to thoughtfulness, he's all there. I can't wait to see him again. I'm no clearer on my sexual agenda, but am learning to live with the uncertainty.

THE HEART OF A CANDIDATE

May 17
After viewing *Braveheart* several more times over the weekend and being reminded of my warlike Scottish heritage, I've come up with an idea for the talent show. We Scots may not come out the winner

in every battle, or even most battles, but we are very tough nonetheless. What was needed was a demonstration of my ancestral qualities.

Shawn didn't seem to understand at first what I was asking.

"I need a talent, for this talent show. For the Miss Smithers. And I thought maybe I could use my katas and all that, you know, for my talent."

Then I turned on the salesmanship.

"I know it sounds sort of strange. But it's not really. Martial arts are as much a talent as baton toss or twirling."

"Shit, yeah," said Jeff, who stood listening. He was outraged at the thought that anyone might think differently. "Like the sword work. I'd like to see one of those twirler girls try that shit with a pair of kung fu knives."

Shawn ignored him, and I continued at my most persuasive.

"I think it would be good advertisement for the dojo. Probably bring in a few more students."

Shawn thought for a moment.

"Is this important to you?"

"Yes."

"You are part of this dojo. We will do what's best for you. I just want you to remember that there's a reason the tests are usually private."

I nodded eagerly.

"Okay. I will prepare your test and administer it on the night of your contest. Make sure your gi is clean. You are representing the club in public."

And that was it.

May 20

I don't know if I can take another workout with Jeff. He's decided that we have to practice together every day to get me ready for the talent show. He says Shawn might "throw the book" at me and that I have to be "ready for damn near anything." And then he gets into these reminiscences about his past martial-arts tests. The proudest moments of his life, he says, have been when he's passed those tests. Then he asks how I plan to wear my hair for the talent show and whether I've given some thought to getting it cut.

I'm trying to get up the nerve to tell him about Goose. I just hate to hurt his feelings. I feel like I'm in a love triangle that consists of a girl who likes a boy who likes her back and then some other guy who talks all the time and sometimes gets punched.

314

As if that wasn't bad enough, I go home to find my dad and the rest of "the old band" practicing and auditioning various barflies from the Legion and other talent hot spots.

My dad's band consists of him and his two friends Lyle and Matt. Lyle and Matt are more functional than the Geniuses, but just barely. They play guitar and drums respectively, and sing a bit. As I said, the three of them used to be in a band called the Hoar Hounds that was quite popular around the north at some unimaginable point in the distant past. They always felt ripped off that they never "broke out" the way Chilliwack and Trooper and BTO did. Those were apparently very popular bands that people back then had heard of.

The disappointment was hard to take, but they still had some good times, which they lose no opportunity to talk about at length. The Geniuses have been sitting in on what everyone is now calling "the sessions," as though more than just idle gossip and caterwauling is taking place. Finn, Kelly, and Marcus are beginning to display signs of jealousy that my dad has other friends to play with. Finn is handling it best, because he is focused on me and my talent competition and every day asks to see a few high blocks and discuss my strategy to "crush the competition." But Kelly and Marcus don't have anything to distract them, so now they sit downstairs, sulking and sighing, when Dad, Matt, and Lyle talk about being "on the road" back in the day. But for whatever reason, the Geniuses refuse to miss a single minute of the sessions or the unfailingly awful auditions. No luck finding another band member yet, but the standards are not high, so it shouldn't be long.

Even though they don't practice while he is working, Mr. Polaski finds the thought of the band in his space intolerable. He says my father's friends move things and "stink the place up," and he is becoming increasingly unhappy. My father doesn't seem to mind and has begun moving the sessions closer and closer to Mr. P.'s work hours. Mr. Polaski's face is frightening when he is passed on the stairs by the Geniuses and whatever deadbeat is currently trying out for the band. My dad should be more careful. The family business has gotten a lot more profitable since we got a productive employee. We wouldn't want to lose him.

Bob is probably the most anxious of anyone about the talent show. My last session he sent me home with a three-foot-high stack of books on maintaining self-esteem in the face of defeat. That was very reassuring.

"It's not that I don't think you'll do well," he said, in his intimate growl. "But on the off chance that, well, you know, something goes wrong, it's good to be prepared."

He has no faith. Either that or he knows me really well.

My mother's been working the phones trying to get the goods on the competition. This is the same woman who was against the whole enterprise not long ago. No wonder I'm so inconsistent.

When I walked into the kitchen tonight after practice, she wasted no time with preliminaries.

"Geraldine told me the Chus have a trampoline. Are you ready for that?" she demanded.

"What?"

She spoke slowly. "The Chus have a trampoline. That means that Zelda, what's her name there, you know, Miss Forest Products, has a *trampoline*. Geraldine lives next door to the Chus, and she say's Zelda's been out there every night for a week."

Mother paused and stared at me significantly.

"Zelda can do a backflip."

I just stared back. What was I supposed to do

about Zelda's ability to do a backflip? Go over to her house and shoot her off the tramp in mid tumble? Hope that the incontinence trampolinists often get catches up with her sooner rather than later? I should have known that once my mother got involved in the pageant, she'd go crazy. It's almost enough to make me miss the days when she didn't care.

May 22

The Hoar Hounds have found the new band member. Her name is Betty Lou and she used to be in punk bands until she moved to Smithers to run a roadside produce stand. It didn't take her long to discover that the growing season here lasts only two months, and therefore her work season is only about a week in the height of summer. She added tree planting to her résumé, and since that is quite seasonal also, she has a lot of free time on her hands, which she spends drinking quietly in the Legion.

Betty Lou has a black helmet of hair with very short bangs that make her eyes look permanently startled. She is liberally tattooed and even in winter wears tank tops under her overalls to show off the snakes that run up and down her arms. She is quite possibly the coolest person I've ever seen.

318

The Hoar Hounds had almost given up on finding someone. They'd auditioned pretty much every regular in the Legion and the Curling Club without success. Then the bartender at the Legion told Finn that he thought he'd seen Betty Lou using a guitar case to display zucchinis last year. Finn investigated further and discovered that she used to be in bands. Somehow he convinced her that the Hoar Hounds would be a fun gig.

My father, Matt, and Lyle looked intimidated when Betty Lou appeared in our basement with Finn. When they kicked off a song and she tore into it with punk rock abandon, they looked even more terrified. Suddenly all their songs were about half as long and twice as fast, which is a definite improvement. Betty Lou gives the Hoar Hound sound a much-needed boost of energy. I am quite inspired by Betty Lou and may ask her where she gets her tattoos done. Who knows—there might be time to get one before the Sweetheart Ball.

Later

Betty Lou was the last straw for Mr. Polaski. He made some comment to her as he was leaving and she was arriving this afternoon, and she stuck out her pierced tongue at him. I could hear the scream from my bedroom upstairs.

"Jaysus Keyrighst! What the hell's wrong with her goddamn tongue?"

The male Hoar Hounds and their sad little contingent of groupies all laughed, as though they felt much more confident around Betty Lou than they really do, and Mr. Polaski stormed out.

Dad should really be more careful with Mr. Polaski's feelings.

On a more personal note, Goose is coming for the Sweetheart Ball! This time we're going to work on my 'zine together, and who knows what else we'll get up to.

I haven't really thought much about the end of the pageant. To be honest, I'm not expecting to win. Sure, it's possible. All the judges could strike a blow for mediocrity and vote for me. It would be a tribute to all those people everywhere who aren't the best or the worst or even the strangest and never will be. But I'm not holding my breath.

My mother is another story. She was on the phone again tonight. This time she was talking to her friend Pit, so named for her copious quantities of underarm hair. Mother was telling Pit that she heard that Mrs. Bell, Miss Northern Real Estate's mom, has been working day and night to finance her daughter's candidacy.

"The four-hundred-dollar clothing allowance wasn't enough," said Mother disdainfully. "No, nowhere near enough. I heard they ordered Sandra's dress for the Sweetheart Ball from Holt Renfrew. A thousand dollars. It's obscene. It really is. This thing isn't supposed to be about the money."

She listened into the receiver, and then said, "Oh no. It isn't a beauty contest. There's no way I would let Alice be in one of those. No, this is more about citizenship, really. Which is why it's so offensive that some people are trying to buy the crown."

May 24

Mr. Polaski quit today. He left my mother a note saying there was more to life than money and he couldn't have anything to do with that freak show we call a basement anymore. He wrote that if he wanted to rub elbows with the painted lady he'd go to the circus, and if he wanted lazy he'd get a cat. Mr. Polaski left school at a young age, which would explain his difficulty in expressing himself in print.

My mother was quite annoyed with my dad, but

he had a plan. He's hired Betty Lou to do candles. She is apparently an experienced craftsperson and knows about candles, although I heard Finn whisper to Marcus that he doesn't think dripping hot wax on people for kicks really counts. Betty Lou scares Dad almost as much as Mr. P. did, so it will be interesting to see how this works out. But my mom loves Betty Lou and says it's good for me to have another strong woman in the house as a role model. You've got to hand it to my mom—she doesn't scare easy.

My dad probably would have been in a lot more trouble over Mr. Polaski if my mom hadn't been distracted by the talent show tomorrow. There is really nothing she can do to help me, and it's driving her crazy. When I asked if she was actually going to come to watch, she looked at me like I was crazy.

"Of course I'll be there."

"But I thought you don't agree with the Miss Smithers."

She made a dismissive noise with her tongue.

"Parents support their children, regardless of their feelings. You will understand when you have kids."

STAY CALM AND KEEP YOUR HANDS UP

May 25

Oh my God, I am so nervous. We have to leave for the Legion in half an hour. You'd think they could find other places in town to hold these stupid events. Are we being groomed to become self-confident young citizens at home in front of a crowd, or barmaids? I mean really.

I'm wearing my leather pants. I need to have at least one positive experience in these things and am praying this might be it. After all, they cost a lot of money.

I've slicked back my hair, partly to try and get it under control and partly to get a Linda-Hamilton-in-*The Terminator* look. (Minus the muscles, obviously.) When he saw me, Finn shook his head and said I looked like one of the boys down at the leather bar. Whatever. I'll just add a bit more lipstick.

I'm going to change into my gi before I start my

routine, but I want to establish a tough-looking image right off.

The whole family is pacing around the house except for MacGregor, who is reading. Finn came over at four and has been drinking heavily to help him with his nerves. I'm glad I've learned my lesson about drinking to deal with difficult situations. I may be nervous, but I don't want to end the night with another geriatric boyfriend.

It would be easier to be confident if I could get my mother to dress in more structured clothing. Really, would it kill her to wear a nice tailored suit? Is there not some law that regulates how much tie-dye a grown woman is allowed to wear? Oh well, I should just be grateful that she's stopped wearing that Che Guevara bandanna that smells like pepper spray.

I don't think I can handle this. What if Shawn beats me up as part of my test? What if he flunks me in front of everyone? I am sick.

I talked to Goose on the phone for moral support, and even he couldn't help ease the dread that's overwhelming me.

Later

I don't think the word *triumph* would be out of place in describing the events of the evening.

Each candidate sat with her family in the audience. It looked like an elementary school play with girls running everywhere in glittering costumes, and parents looking sick with nerves. Zelda's dad, Mr. Chu, stood off to the side of the hall clutching a portable trampoline. Miss Loggers' Association and her parents were on their knees trying to calm a pair of border collies. Other girls held tambourines and juggling sticks. I had no props, except for my gi in a bag at my feet.

Everyone in my entourage fidgeted and fretted through the beginning of the talent show. Finn began groaning loudly and with alarming regularity as soon as we sat down, apparently some stress reaction he has developed that has forced him to take a more relaxed approach to life and make sure his work week never goes beyond three days. He actually threw off several of the competitors with his noises, including Miss 4-H. She was so startled by one of his explosions that she dropped one of the pieces of the bridle that she was trying to put together while blindfolded. She couldn't find it again, and her talent was ruined. I'm not sure how applicable it was to everyday life, anyway.

I went to the washroom to change into my gi, and when I came back, Shawn was there in all his white-pajamaed glory. Amazingly, he was accompanied by every member of our club, from the littlest Butterfly to the biggest Bear, all of whom wore spotless white gis. They filed in and stood against the back of the hall, hands folded in front of them.

When my name was called, I walked to the side of the stage, where Shawn came to meet me. Mrs. Martin spoke into the microphone.

"Tonight Alice MacLeod is going to demonstrate an entry-level martial-arts program with the help of her instructor, Shawn Henry."

Shawn and I climbed up the stairs and onto the stage. He turned to face me. Then he bowed and got into meditation position on his knees, feet tucked under him. I copied him as exactly as I could.

We meditated for a full three minutes. After one minute I could hear the audience begin to shift in their seats. After two minutes I could hear grumbling. By the third minute the audience spoke to each other as though we weren't doing anything up onstage at all. People have no appreciation for the spiritual side of athletics.

At last Shawn clapped his hands, sprang to his feet, and got into a stance. I followed.

He called out the moves of my kata:

"High block."

Up went my arm.

"Low block."

Down went my arm.

Turn. Side block. Kick.

Then he began to work with me so his attack was defended by my moves. Back and forth we went, my blocks repelling him, his thwarting mine.

And then he called a stop, bowed, and went to retrieve something from one of the Bees, who stood poised by the side of the stage.

Shawn came back with two mouth guards, one still wrapped in its package, and two sets of sparring gloves, and handed me one of each. He *was* going to beat me up! And just when it had been going so well.

Before we began, he leaned close and whispered: "Keep your hands up. And don't get mad."

He moved around me and began taking shots at my head. Shot, block, shot, block.

He kicked and made contact, but I didn't move my eyes off his face or let my guard drop.

We sparred back and forth, and then he hit me. It wasn't too hard, but my head snapped back and rage and fear surged through me. He hit me again and tears filled my eyes. I hated him. I wanted to run off the stage. I saw my dad get out of his chair, ready to break it up, but Finn held him back by the shoulder. Another hit, this one connecting with my cheek. I wanted to scream, "Leave me alone," but then I remembered Shawn's words: Keep your hands up and don't get mad.

Another jab, but this time I blocked it. And then I took a chance: I hit him. And I scored! I hit Shawn!

He nodded slightly, and I think his mouth guard might have hidden a small smile.

And then it was over. He stood still and clasped his gloves in front of me. He bowed, and I bowed back.

I'd survived. Shawn hadn't pulverized me.

He asked me four questions about the names of the movements we'd been doing. Then he stood back and said, "Alice MacLeod. I am pleased to welcome you to the intermediate group of K. A. Martial Arts."

At the news my mother shot out of her seat, Finn exploded in some kind of guttural noise one more time, and my dad and MacGregor hugged each other. The rest of the crowd clapped too. When I came down the stairs, everyone from the dojo gathered round to shake my hand and give me a hug. Jeff, suddenly shy, hung back until I said, "Thanks." Then he grabbed me in a bear hug, which took a greater physical toll on me than the entire test with Shawn had.

I don't know how they score the talent part of the Miss Smithers—you know, whether it's a pass/fail or what—but I do know that it was one of my best moments ever.

Esther, Nancy, Melinda, and Mary all came over to congratulate me. Even Miss Loggers' Association and Miss Main Street and a few of the other candidates came over to tell me they thought my routine was "interesting." It could have just been the physical intimidation factor, but I don't think so. They seemed genuinely impressed. My family and Finn were more or less gibbering with pride on the drive home. Like I say, it was a high point. I'm so happy I feel almost whole.

May 27

Yesterday was groundbreaking on many fronts.

The Hoar Hounds have gotten a gig. And wouldn't you know it, the gig is the Sweetheart Ball. I'm sure this is Finn's work. The Hounds have been practicing their Doors songs, and Betty Lou has taught them several songs by a band called Sleater Kinney in which she wails and they look confused. Those songs are only about two minutes long, but they take a lot out of the older members. I am just grateful that by the time they take the stage, the pageant will be over and my father's performance won't be able to hurt my chances.

I finally told Jeff after practice that I couldn't go out with him because my heart belongs to my writing. What I didn't tell him is that my virginity belongs to Goose. He seemed okay with the news, which I thought would have devastated him, because he and almost all the other boys in our dojo have developed an obsession with Betty Lou. They've started hanging around our house pretending to visit with me but actually waiting to see her and carry her guitar case, and ask her questions about what it's like in Toronto.

I'd imagine Jeff is quite torn up but is hiding it

well. He is a Bear after all and trained in the art of self-control.

Karen stopped by unexpectedly, and she was sober.

"I heard about the talent show. Word is your thing was very cool," she said.

Word? There was a word about me?

At first I was nervous to have her in the house unexpectedly. One likes to be prepared for these things. But she set me at ease right away.

She was in Karen casual wear, a matching track suit and brilliant white runners, hair in a ponytail. She charmed my mother by complimenting her on the "energy" in our house, smiled at my dad and his friends as though they were old school chums, and then suggested I get us a cup of tea. I paid close attention to everything she did, figuring it was a lesson in what true social skills look like.

Before I knew it, we were having a conversation that wasn't even slightly awkward. I found myself telling her about Goose and how confusing things were sometimes.

Before she could say anything, we were interrupted by a knock on my door.

"Come in," I said, and the door swung open to

reveal George, her face splotchy and swollen as though she'd been crying. My mother stood behind her looking concerned.

George caught sight of Karen sitting in the chair at my desk.

"You've got company," she said, and took a step back.

"No, it's okay. We're just talking."

As George came into the room, I looked at my mom and nodded and she closed the door.

George sat on the edge of the bed and immediately erupted into tears.

"We broke up," she cried. "He broke up with me."

She sounded destroyed. I couldn't believe this was my ultrastoic friend. I didn't know what to say, but Karen did.

"Bastard," she said automatically. "The damned bastard."

Georgette looked at her gratefully and continued. "I know the relationship was just based on sex. We had it four times. And now he's got someone else. And she's not in 4-H. She's in Pony Club, and they're all so snotty."

"Asshole." Karen nodded.

Taking my cue from her, I added, "Jerk."

By the end of the visit George had calmed down enough to tell us how, on the one hand, she didn't even like him that much. He had started calling her all the time to complain about his parents and how his cow wasn't putting on weight like he'd hoped.

"But *I* was supposed to break up with *him*," she said, disbelief in her voice. "How could he break up with me?"

We established, with Karen's help, that he was a very troubled person and would live to regret the day he'd let George get away.

"Let's face it," said Karen, "the guy's a loser. Before you know it, he'll be crawling back to you on his hands and knees. And if he doesn't, there's something seriously wrong with him."

"Really?" sniffed George.

"Absolutely," said Karen.

Before she left to drive the truck, which she'd taken without permission, back to Houston, George apologized for neglecting our friendship, and I forgave her. We didn't mention my jealousy. It didn't seem relevant.

This is going to sound terrible, but there was something very satisfying about the whole thing. It may have been one of my favorite afternoons ever and not just because George and I are friends again. There was something about consoling George that was really fun. And not only that, her being so upset made me feel sort of superior, or at least needed. I must be a truly terrible person to enjoy a friend's misfortune. But when Karen got up to go, she said about George, "Poor kid," and I could tell she sort of enjoyed the whole thing too. Friendship is a mysterious thing.

THE FINAL ANALYSIS

May 29

I can't say I was exactly surprised when Goose didn't show up for the ball.

"You want to wait a few more minutes?" Mom asked.

Thinking of George, I said, "No. Let's just go."

Mom taped directions to the Legion on the front door, "Just in case he's late," and I dragged myself out to the car.

I did my best to show I didn't care about any of it when Finn led me around the Legion's perimeter with the rest of the girls and their escorts, like so many colts at auction, during the parade of candidates.

When I got up to the podium, I kept my thank-yous to my sponsors and supporters brief and tried not to keep staring over at the door.

I wore my eBay Chinese dress, which I love but may have looked a bit too understated next to some of the other girls' elaborate televised-award-ceremony type dresses.

When Mrs. Martin got up in her sequined sweater set to say how much she'd enjoyed working with us, but had decided to retire as pageant chaperone next year, I didn't take it personally.

They began to announce the winners. Sitting up there on the stage with the other candidates, I confess to a moment of thinking I might have got runner-up or special mention for talent or something. But mostly I concentrated on keeping my face under control. Because the worst thing about losing is when you don't care, but people think you do. So they treat you like a loser, even though you aren't one really, because you don't care, if you see what I mean.

"For the title of Miss Congeniality, we have a surprise tie! Miss 4-H, Penny Higgins, and Miss Main Street, Kathy Richards!"

They got up, squealing and hugging each other.

"And our Princess tonight, runner-up for the

title of Miss Smithers, is Miss Deschooling, Mary Peters."

Mary smiled shyly, and we all clapped for her, and then she gave a very coherent three-sentence speech, showing how far she'd come from her mute beginnings.

"Drum roll please. And the Miss Smithers crown goes to: Miss Ski Smithers! Esther Valgardson!"

Esther rose gracefully, looking fabulous and elegant in a floor-length rose-pink dress with spaghetti straps. She didn't forget anyone in her acceptance speech, even her sister, whom I could see sitting with her parents, hunched over and glowering up at the stage.

Looking at Esther's sister, I had a flash that being perfect had its drawbacks as well.

So I didn't win the Miss Smithers contest. Of course Esther did. And Mary came in second. That's the whole point of a competition like this. It's all about reaffirming what we already know about where we stand in the social strata of the town. Nice, luminous, religious people like Esther win the Miss Smithers contests of the world. Cheating connivers like Miss Frontage Road don't. Neither do thrift-store freaks like me, but at least I knew I wouldn't win. I saw Gina, Miss Bulkley Valley Fall Fair, actually crying as the winner was announced. As far as I'm concerned, that kind of disappointment is worse than the loss of any contest.

And sometimes people actually recognize substance over style, as the coaward for niceness to Miss Main Street shows.

The thing that made me mad, though, was that after we got offstage, people insisted on treating me like I was devastated. My mom took the loss personally. After she gave me a bone-crushing fierce mother hug, she and Miss Chicken Creek's mother started discussing in whispers their theory that the whole thing was fixed.

Seeing our mothers together, Nancy came over with her boyfriend in tow and said, "Now that this thing is done, we should hang out sometime." I nodded and smiled and tried not to look as dateless as I felt.

Bob acted as though every hope I'd ever had for a happy life had died with the loss.

"Alice?" he ventured. "You okay?"

Betty Lou, who is apparently dating him, assessed the situation with her giant, kohl-rimmed eyes. "Come on, Bob," she said, "help me get set up."

The only people who seemed to understand that I didn't care were Finn and Karen. Finn walked up to me after the ceremony, new boyfriend in tow. He gave me a kiss and said my dress looked fantastic. "Almost as good as those leather pants," he said with a wink. When his boyfriend, a chiropractor from Prince Rupert, said something to me in soothing tones, Finn shushed him and said, "None of that. As if she cares. It's about the clothes, sweetheart." Exactly.

When Karen stopped in at the dance with her date, a counselor in the local treatment center (part of her plan to cut down on her drinking), she gave me a big hug. I felt like I had to explain, so I told her who won. "Miss Ski Smithers took it. Miss Deschooling second. Miss Main Street and Miss 4-H got nicest."

She nodded thoughtfully and said, "Yeah. That seems about right."

I know she noticed that Goose wasn't there, but she didn't say anything.

God, she's cool.

MacGregor brought a friend from his science club. She is apparently a fellow newt aficionado. She is about ten years old, and she wore inadvertently hip glasses that made her look like a tiny junior in an Ivy

League school. I considered warning her that if she hurts my little brother, I'd be forced to kill all her newts, but one look at her told me that the worst she was likely to do was forget to thank him enough in her acceptance speech for curing cancer at age fifteen.

"Alice, this is Bernice," Mac introduced her.

"How do you do?" I asked, feeling the need to be formal in the face of such a serious-looking girl.

"Fine, thank you," said Bernice, pushing her glasses back up her nose. "I enjoyed the evening very much."

"It's not over yet," said MacGregor, and then added a bit shyly, "Our dad is playing the music."

"You have a very talented family," commented Bernice with no apparent irony.

"Thanks," said MacGregor, and then they went back to sit at our table.

After I snarled at them a few times, the rest of my group—Marcus and Kelly—stopped consoling me and started dancing. My dad and the Hoar Hounds weren't bad at all, and in a perfect touch, Betty Lou brought a friend of hers who plays the bagpipes. No Scot can be a total loser when the bagpipes are playing. I danced a couple of times, but I have to admit that my heart wasn't in it.

Then, as I was sitting alone at our table, I saw the front door open and Goose stumbled in, looking disheveled in a brown suit and crooked bow tie.

He saw me right away, and for some reason I felt like crying. Love is so dumb.

He came and stood by the table and I just sat there, feeling totally overwhelmed and awkward.

"You look amazing. Really, really great. I'm sorry I'm late," he apologized. "Did you win?" he asked, as though it was seriously a possibility.

I shook my head.

"You should have," he said, and I know he meant it.

It turned out he'd had a flat tire, so he had to abandon his truck and hitch a ride. The truth is that I never really doubted he'd show up eventually. He might have had the day wrong or an accident on the way, but I knew he'd make it.

We danced and danced with Bernice and Mac, and Mom and Marcus and Kelly and Finn and his boyfriend and Karen and hers. And I felt proud to be with Goose. He looked great. He cut off most of his hair in order to save time in the morning, and he's so blond he looks almost bald. He still had that way of smiling at me that made me feel like there was someone beautiful standing right behind me.

If he's not too tired, tonight may be the night. Or maybe tomorrow will be the day. Either way, Goose and I are going to do it.

This may have been a big night for Miss Ski Smithers, but in the final assessment, I think Miss Rod & Gun Club is going to be the winner.

May 30

Deep Inside Miss Smithers IV: The Final Analysis

This year's pageant is done, and another group of worthy young women have proved themselves able to withstand the rigors of the very demanding contest. There's been a lot of growth among the candidates, and the new scores reflect that.

Congratulations, girls. It's a wrap.

COMPETITOR	BEAUTY	TALENT	CONGE-NIALITY	FASHION SENSE	COMMENTS
Miss 4-H (Penny Higgins) (crowned Miss Congeniality)	7	7	9	6	Candidate really was quite nice. And not in a fake way. Deserved title.
Miss Northern Real Estate (Sandra Bell)	7	9	9	7	Candidate made a lot of improvement. Tap dancing and whistling at the same time gave her impressive gains in the talent category.
Miss Main Street (Kathy Richards) (crowned Miss Congeniality)	7	7	8	6	Initially crusty demeanor hides a warm heart. Color us surprised!
Miss Panelboard Plant (Melissa Vanderhaan)	7	7	7	6	Candidate's piercing was a bold move. Too bold for the judges? Still, kudos for courage.
Miss Deschooling (Mary Peters) (Runner-Up)	8	8	8	8	Candidate has shown strength, courage, and resilience. And to the delight of some, the dread white bikini!

COMPETITOR	BEAUTY	TALENT	CONGE-NIALITY	FASHION SENSE	COMMENTS
Miss Loggers' Association (Debbie White)	7	7	7	6	Candidate's hangover recipe really works!
Miss Ski Smithers (Esther Valgardson) (crowned Miss Smithers)	8	8	8	8	Really among the finest examples of a citizen and a Young Christian you could ask for.
Miss Forest Products (Zelda Chu)	7	7	7	8	Another piercing and she'll have trouble getting through a metal detector. Should beware of potential harmful effect of excessive trampoline use.
Miss Frontage Road (Jasmine Davis)	1	1	1	1	Nepotism isn't just a suburb of Ottawa, is it, Mrs. Davis, aka Librarian of the Damned? Best we can say is that candidate comes by her devious nature honestly.
Miss Evelyn Station Fish Hatchery (Ingrid Ricci)	7	6	6	6	Handled a difficult fashion show outfit with aplomb. Not many other people could make a kickboat look attractive. Intriguing speech about the life cycle of the endangered spotted owl suggests hidden depths.

COMPETITOR	BEAUTY	TALENT	CONGE-NIALITY	FASHION SENSE	COMMENTS
Miss Chicken Creek Fire Department (Nancy Morton)	8	7	9	8	She's cynical. She's got a weird sponsorship name. We love her!
Miss Bulkley Valley Fall Fair (Gina Wilson)	6	6	6	6	Candidate must be admired for attempts to perpetrate graft and other crimes of insinuation. Looks like she's got a bright future in politics in front of her!
Miss Moricetown (Melinda Joseph)	6	6	8	7	Candidate is not only tough but kind also. Look out, world! This girl's going to change some things!
Miss Rod & Gun Club (Alice MacLeod)	7	8	9	8	Candidate is a promising martial artist but really needs to develop a new strategy for intimacy with boyfriend. At current rate may be too old to have intimate relations by the time she actually succeeds in getting him alone.